Tales of a

Substitute Teacher

Volume 2: A Magician's Tricks Take Over Room 6

By: SHERI POWROZEK

D1056379

This is a work of fiction. Names, characters, places, and incidents either are the products of the author's imagination or are used fictitiously. Any resemblance to actual persons, living or dead, businesses, companies, events, or locales is entirely coincidental.

Mr. Miagi and *Karate Kid* is a trademark of the 1984 film written by Robert Mark Kamen; Lego Ninjago (Master Wu, Zane, Sushi Chef, and Misako) is a trademark of The Lego Group; "Deep in the Heart of Texas" is a song written in 1941 by June Hershey and Don Swander; *Starry Night, Self-Portrait with a Straw Hat,* and *Self-Portrait with Bandaged Ear* are paintings by Vincent van Gogh; Vincent Willem van Gogh was a Dutch Post-Impressionist painter who is among the most famous and influential figures in the history of Western art. Doritos and Cheetos were created by Frito Lay, and are owned and trademarked by Pepsi Co.; Gatorade is owned by PepsiCo (owned by Quaker Oats Company and trademarked as Stokely-Van Camp); YouTube was created by Chad Hurley, Steve Chen, and Jawed Karim. It was sold to Google and is owned by Alphabet Inc.; Prodigy (Smart Teacher Inc.) is aligned with Ontario Curriculum & Common Core; Harry Potter, Albus Dumbledore, and Hogwarts are trademarks of the book series and films of *Harry Potter* written by J.K. Rowling; *Clash of Clans* and "The Wizard Song" is a trademark of Supercell, developed and published by Finnish; *Charlotte's Web* is a 2006 film based on the 1952 novel by E.B. White; Superman is a trademark of DC Comics, created by writer Jerry Siegel and artist Joe Shuster; *Sleeping Beauty* and Disney are trademarks of The Walt Disney Company; AC/DC is an Australian rock band formed in 1973 by Malcolm and Angus Young (made up of : Brian Johnson, Malcolm Young, Phil Rudd, Angus Young, and Cliff Williams); Xtramath (a Seattle non-profit) started in 2007 by David Jeschke; Aaron Rodgers, Odell Beckham, Leveon Bell, Antonio Brown, and Tom Brady are NFL players; "Twinkle, Twinkle Little Star" is an English lullaby written in the 19th-century and the lyrics are from a poem by Jane Taylor; "Hot Cross Buns" is an English nursery rhyme published in 1798 (songwriter unknown); "Mary Had a Little Lamb" is an English nursery rhyme published by Marsh, Capen & Lyon, originally a poem by Sarah Josepha Hale; Michael Jordan is an American retired professional basketball player, businessman, and principal owner and chairman of the Charlotte Hornets of the National Basketball Association; ESPN is a U.S.-based global cable and satellite sports television channel owned by ESPN Inc., a joint venture owned by The Walt Disney Company and Hearst Communications; Xbox is a video gaming brand created and owned by Microsoft.

DEDICATION

This book is dedicated to my family and all the students that inspired me during my time as a substitute teacher. Each child that I had the privilege of working with, left a footprint on my heart, and I will forever remember them.

To my husband, Shane, who constantly pushes me to fulfill my dreams and supports me in all that I do. And to my children, Chase and Reese, who are my heart's breath and make everything so much brighter, filling my life with joy and happiness.

TABLE OF CONTENTS

CHAPTER 1: FIRST DAY JITTERS

"Mom, what's the weather like?" I asked, yelling across the house, wondering if I should wear pants or shorts.

"I think it's supposed to be in the seventies today, but right now it's only fifty-something. Why don't you go out the front door and check? You should probably bring a sweatshirt with you. The rule last year was that you had to have a coat or sweatshirt with you if it was fifty or below," Mom replied.

"It's not like they are going to say something on the first day. Besides, it's August," I said, shaking my head and smiling over her worrying.

"Okay. But the weather is a little weird this week. I think storms are supposed to blow through and then it's supposed to warm back up next week," she yelled back.

"Ugh. Tornado weather." I sighed.

In my room, rummaging through clothes, I picked up a neon green dry-fit baseball shirt, matching athletic shorts, and long black basketball socks. Quickly changing, I then grabbed a sweatshirt from a hanger in the closet and walked out of my room, closing the door behind me. Heading into the bathroom, I dashed past the mirror and swiped my hair up to the right to fix the droopiness of my overgrown spiked mohawk.

"We really should have gotten your hair cut this weekend!" Mom yelled from the kitchen.

"It's fine," I said.

"You want to look decent for your first day of school, don't you?" she asked.

"Eh, no one cares."

Mom darted me her normal look of confusion over my nonchalant, whatever attitude.

"Okay then," she said tiredly. "I packed your lunch and charged your computer. They are sitting on the counter in the laundry room."

"Awe. I kind of wanted hot lunch today," I said with a disappointed tone.

"Honey, I asked you yesterday, were you not listening?" Mom smiled and raised her eyebrow at me.

I blushed and gave her my guilty look. "I don't remember, sorry." I smiled and then giggled.

"Are you a little nervous for your first day of fifth grade? You are the big kahuna this year, the oldest in the school. You will have to be extra responsible and helpful to the younger ones, okay?" she insisted.

"I know, Mom," I responded, talking softly.

I was still trying to wake up fully. After a long summer of sleeping in, I wasn't used to being up so early. I couldn't concentrate on her lecture about maturity. I kept thinking about what bus seat I wanted and who would be in my class this year. My older brother, Will, zipped around the corner of the kitchen and playfully punched me in my arm, antagonizing me. I quickly snapped back and grabbed ahold of him with a full body tackle, knocking over the kitchen stool.

"Boys, knock it off!" Mom yelled.

Turning towards my brother with urgency, she bent over and pulled back gently on his shoulder. "Come on, Will, you are going to be late. You should already be on your way. Quit picking on your brother," she said.

"I'm going to skip school today. I'm busy knocking some sense into this kid," Will said sarcastically, with a sinister tone.

Will started laughing and flipped me over. His height and weight were triple mine, but I wasn't willing to let go. He laid across the top of me and put me in a wrestling hold, locking me to the ground.

"Say mercy!" Will yelled in my ear.

"No!" I yelled back, turning bright red. Letting out a big sigh, I used all my might to push back. Starting to pant from the pressure of him being on top of me, I pushed up with my arms and grunted.

"Ok, ok...enough. Get up," Mom said, pushing herself in between us and prying our bodies apart, worried that I would stop breathing.

Mom grabbed the hood of Will's sweatshirt and stood between us. "Can't we have one morning without the two of you fighting and acting like animals? Frankie, you're a mess now, look at you. Run into the bathroom and straighten yourself up. Did you brush your teeth yet? You are going to be late, the bus will be here in two minutes and you are not even outside."

I looked at the clock and noticed she was right. I was going to be late.

"Mom I have to go. I have to go," I said insistently going into a mad rush. I grabbed my stuff off the counter and ran to put my shoes on.

"Well, did you do the things I just said? I will drive you if you didn't. I don't want you to have stinky breath," Mom said, laughing and plugging her nose, to make her joke known.

"Yes, Mom. Don't worry." I flashed her a smile and showed her my teeth.

Setting her attention back on my brother, she was irritated with his slow-moving nature.

"Will, it's not a good look for you to be irresponsible on the first day of school either. Just because you are in high school doesn't mean you can go in whenever you want to," she said.

Will looked at her with loving eyes, scooted over by her, and gave her a noogie. "I have ten minutes. It is right down the street. Are you trying to get rid of me?" he asked with a goofy grin.

Mom put her arm around him and gave him a tight squeeze. "Maybe." Mom looked at him and laughed. "No. I'm just kidding. Never. I wish you could stay with me always. But then I would never get anything done," she said in an exaggerated tone. "Please don't drive fast. Just leave your brother alone from now on in the morning, okay? I love you."

Will leaned over and placed a kiss upon her head. "I have study hall first thing in the morning, so I'll text you. I don't want you worrying about me all day. I know you...You are going to be nervous, thinking I got my first tardy."

"Bye," Mom said kindly, with a smile.

Will walked out and waved at me as he got in his pick-up truck, sticking out his tongue. "Bye, F-money!"

Ugh. I really don't like it when he calls me that. I scrunched my nose at him and waved. "Bye, Willy Wonker," I joked.

Will beeped his horn and made me jump. I took the basketball that was sitting in the grass and threw it close to his car. I knew it wouldn't hit him, but I wanted to scare him. Then, the bus appeared from around the bend. I picked up the basketball and threw a three-point shot. *Yes! It went in! I'm such a baller!* I jumped up and down and then made my way to the end of the driveway.

Mom ran outside. "Bye! Have a good day! Love you, Frankie."

"Love you, Mom," I said back.

"Be the best fifth grader you can be. Remember to be kind and listen to your teacher!" she yelled.

Mrs. Suzanne waved me across the road and I walked up the stairs of the bus.

"Hello there, Frankie. Don't you look mighty tan from the summer sun."

"I wish it was warmer today," I said back to her.

"I know. There is such a weird chill in the air for being the end of August. How was your summer?" she asked.

"It was good. It's hard to come back," I said.

"I hear ya. I could use another pool day," Mrs. Suzanne said cheerily. She turned around and pointed. "Pick whatever seat you want except the first three rows, that's for the kindergartners and the first graders."

Being in 5th grade meant I got to sit in the very back, in the last row, looking out the exit window. I have been waiting to grab that seat for the longest time. The last two years Billy Johnston had it and he wasn't someone you wanted to mess with. He would glare at me any time I even looked at him. I think he knew I wanted his seat. He was off at the middle school now and I wasn't sad about it.

Rushing back, I sat down and put my stuff down next to me. I was excited to see my best friend, Jayden. Usually, I see him on the weekends at baseball and football practice and we have endless sleepovers, but he was gone this summer in Arizona. We like to do the same things and talk about sports. Jayden and I are like walking sports almanacs. After a few stops, we pulled up to his house and waited for a minute, but no one came. I let out a big sigh and huffed. *Where is he?* I didn't want anyone else to sit with me. For the next five stops, I placed my backpack in the open space next to me and stared out the side window, so no one could take it.

Amanda and Marissa sat down in the seat in front of me. Amanda kept looking back through the crack, between the seat and the window. She made a silly face at me.

"Hi!" she squealed in an upbeat, high-pitched voice.

"Hi," I said back in a shy tone.

"What's wrong?" she asked.

"Nothing. I wanted Jayden to come back."

I tried to break eye contact with her, looking out the window, but she was non-stop talking.

"Did you get Mrs. Webber or Mrs. Schubby?" she asked.

"Mrs. Webber." I said.

"So did I. And so did Bobby, Austin, Kristin, Mackenna, and Landon. They had a group chat about it last night. That's all I know so far," she said.

"Cool," I said, in a monotone voice. "I don't have a phone, so I don't get to see those texts."

"You should get one," Amanda said.

"My mom won't let me. She said not until sixth grade." I frowned, thinking about that rule, and looked out the window.

I kept to myself and remained straight-faced. I wasn't in the mood to chat. The girls were being too giggly and silly. Jayden said Amanda had a crush on me. She was nice, but I didn't want to entertain her giddiness so early in the morning. I couldn't wait to get off the bus. After such a long break, I had forgotten my tendency to get motion sickness. Throbbing behind my eyes had already begun and an uneasy stomach left me feeling a bit green. I kept to myself and looked out the window for the last four stops, trying to focus on anything other than the bumping and shaking of the vehicle. We headed down the main interstate for five more miles and then pulled into the parking lot. Seeing school again filled me with nerves. I wasn't sure what to expect for this year, but I feared it was going to be more challenging.

"Frankie, look! It's Jayden. That's his car. He must have been a car rider this morning," said Amanda, pointing towards the parking lot.

I jumped up in excitement, noticing him. He was walking up the sidewalk to the office. "*Yes!*" I yelled out loud, throwing my fist in the air with enthusiasm. I felt immediate relief as the bus pulled to a stop and opened the door. Grabbing my things, I followed everyone off the bus. That was the only downfall of sitting in the last seat. I was the last off and I had to wait for everyone to move.

"Have a good day," Mrs. Suzanne cheerily shouted.

I nodded my head. "You too," I replied.

Taking a few steps down from the bus, I walked on the sidewalk up to the double doors to the entryway. Walking in, I noticed the newly painted walls, full of illustrations of countries and continents from around the world. I couldn't believe this was my last year in elementary. The staff decorated the school with globes, passports, luggage, and other artifacts that had to do with traveling and a banner of "Oh the Places We Will Go" hung, dangling, from one side of the hallway to the other.

I kept my things to my side and fast-walked through the hallways, looking for any sight of the principal so I could move faster. Looking around, checking both sides of the hall, I was in the clear. I started to dash down to the fifth-grade corridor and ran into a little kid from the preschool, knocking him on the ground.

"Oops. Sorry!" I yelled.

He began crying and ran to his teacher. I clenched my teeth, feeling guilty, remembering what my mom said this morning. I could hear her now, 'Be more responsible, Frankie'. Getting to my locker, I hung my backpack on the hook, threw my gym shoes in the top cubby, and took my lunch bag out, to throw in the bin by the door. I saw Mrs. Webber waiting for everyone by the doorway, scanning the hallway and making small talk. She is a younger teacher that has been in the school as an assistant, and always seems so fun. She loves playing sports and games with her students and always has new NFL, MLB, or NBA memorabilia to show off, which I love. *She might even have more than me? Nah, I have a lot!* My friend Miles, from down the road, had her last year. He said that she loves the outdoors and keeps insects and reptiles in the classroom. I secretly wished all summer I would have her, because she seems nice and athletic. As I headed past her to go into the classroom, she stopped me.

"Mr. Smith, I heard we have something in common," said Mrs. Webber.

I looked at her with confusion. "Really?" I asked, furrowing my brows.

"Yep! We both love the Chicago Bears," she said, while smiling.

Bobby came up behind me and interrupted the conversation. "BOOOO! Packers rule."

Mrs. Webber winked at me and laughed. "Okay, boys. Go find your seats."

It is going to be a good year, I can feel it.

We were five minutes into saying the pledge when Jayden walked in. My eyes widened. I smiled and waved at him. Then, another boy followed. The principal came in and stood in the center of the room.

"Class, this is Teddy. Teddy is staying with Jayden and will be attending Moose Academy with all of you. Please make him feel welcome."

"Hi, Teddy!" the class yelled all at once.

"Welcome, Teddy. Hello, Jayden. I'm so glad you are here. How is that throwing arm of yours, Jayden? Have you been practicing this summer?" asked Mrs. Webber.

Mrs. Webber knew Jayden was the best quarterback in the county. He was featured in the local newspaper last year when our team won the Super Bowl.

Embarrassed, Jayden shook his head in a yes motion. "A little."

"You boys can find your desks. We are going to start with an introduction packet," Mrs. Webber said.

Whispering, I tried to get his attention. "Jayden, look." I pulled out two MVP football cards from my pocket.

He opened his mouth in jealousy and excitement. "*Whoa!*"

Mrs. Webber wanted our attention.

"Everyone, look up at the screen. As you will see, fifth grade has a lot of neat things. This year we have amazing learning experiences outside of school. We go to the space museum and we get to have a retreat at Golden Oaks for a few nights. But I want to stress to all of you, it's a crucial year for you guys. Next year you will be middle schoolers. I'm going to give you a lot of responsibility and I expect at this age that you know how to manage your time and organization. Right now, you are used to a smaller school. Next year, most of you will go off to public school, and your classes will be much bigger. It may overwhelm you."

I started to feel a little anxious. I never really thought about the changes I would have to go through. The thought of locker combinations and gym uniforms made me less than thrilled, yet the idea of a little more independence and freedom made it exciting. And I would finally be able to go to school with some of my other friends from baseball and football, that attend other schools in the area. Next year, we will all be together. Mrs. Webber walked up and down the aisles, giving us an instruction sheet.

"Right now, I want all of you to get acquainted with each other. I'm giving you ten minutes to walk around and check out the different centers I have set up. Make sure your desk has all your supplies. I have everything listed on the supply list that I'm passing out and instructions on where to put them. You may talk amongst each other, just keep the conversations school related. If you don't know someone, please introduce yourself. I don't care if you get a little crazy, just don't get out of hand."

I opened my mouth in shock, that she said we could get crazy. That was the first time I had ever heard a teacher say that before. Not that I was a crazy kid, but it was nice to know we didn't have to worry about being quiet.

Jayden ran back to my desk with lots of energy. "Hey! What's up," he said.

"Hey. I didn't know if you were going to be here today. Who is this kid that's staying with you?" I asked.

"He's my cousin. My aunt and uncle are moving back from Arizona, but until they can sell their house they have to stay out there. They wanted Teddy to start school and not switch in the middle of the year, so my mom offered to keep him with us. He's cool. He is not into sports or anything, but you will like him."

Jayden turned to look at Teddy. He was standing all alone, fiddling with his fingers, looking around shyly.

"Teddy come here," Jayden said, waving him over.

Teddy walked over, smiling at Jayden, happy that he wasn't alone.

"This is Frankie. Remember when I was telling you about my best friend?" Jayden asked.

"Yeah. Hi," Teddy said shyly.

"Hi," I said.

Remembering something, I jumped up. "I didn't get to tell you, I got the back row on the bus this year," I said.

"Oh, man. My mom said I have to sit with Teddy. Can he sit with us?" Jayden asked, raising his top lip and eyebrow, unsure of what I might say.

"Sure," I said.

The thoughts in my head weren't nice, but I didn't want three people in our seat. We are going to be scrunched. I didn't know Teddy, but I was kind of sad that I had to share Jayden's time. I pulled my football cards back out and let Jayden look at them.

"*What?!* You got Tom Brady from The Patriots, I want that card!" Jayden exclaimed.

"I know! I couldn't believe it. I figured I wouldn't get it since it was a popular card," I said.

We walked around the room and checked out all the new centers. We had a new science center with butterflies, crickets, a turtle, a salamander, and frogs.

"Awesome!" I said out loud.

"You like frogs and insects, Frankie?" asked Mrs. Webber.

"Yep. I love them. I wanted a pet turtle for my birthday this year, but my mom wouldn't let me," I said.

"I don't know if you know this, but I am an advocate for wildlife awareness and I am very passionate about reptiles and amphibians and trying to keep them safe. I love educating my classes on them," said Mrs. Webber.

"Alligators are my favorite. I saw a bunch in Florida last year and I even got to take one of those airboat tours. One of them came right up to us," I informed.

"That's one pet I haven't had yet." Mrs. Webber laughed.

"Our tour guide told me that they are attracted to white," I continued.

"That is interesting. Thanks for sharing," Mrs. Webber responded.

"EWWWW," Charlotte whined.

"What do you think is gross, Charlotte?" Mrs. Webber asked.

"They are slimy and smelly and dirty. *Yuck.*"

Charlotte was being extra dramatic in front of the other girls in the class, shaking her body around in disgust. There was a loud outburst of comments. "So gross!", "Nasty!", "Keep them away from me!"

"Everyone, gather around me. I want to go over a few of my rules when dealing with our pets. Number one: no matter what you think, even if you think they are the most disgusting creature ever, every living thing on Earth deserves respect and care. So, even if you don't enjoy them as much as I do, I will expect that. Be kind to my pets. Number 2: keep an open mind. My favorite thing is discussing thoughts on this matter. When you first look at them, you probably see their little legs and you can see them crawling around and it might scare you. The important part is that no one has to touch them. You can watch and learn about them. Throughout the year, we will learn many new things about all our pets and I have a feeling you will grow to love them. If not, you will be that much smarter." She smiled and winked at Charlotte.

"I ate frog legs once," Bobby said, as he put his face up to the tank, blowing on the glass with his mouth.

"Hmmm...I don't think my friends will taste very good. Don't get any ideas. And unless you want Amphibianosous Garatosous Disease, you better not put your mouth on there. Who knows what kind of stuff is on there. They are very dirty and filled with bacteria. I would hate for you to get sick." Mrs. Webber widened her eyes at him and then raised the side of her mouth, giving him a silly smile.

"Huh? Amphibia what?" Bobby was confused.

"Is that a real disease?" I asked quietly to Mrs. Webber.

She looked at me, shrugged her shoulders, and then winked. "More like Salmonella bacteria, but we will let him think it over."

I chuckled.

Phil walked over to her. "Mrs. Webber, is it true that you let students bring in insects from recess to stay in the classroom?"

"Phil, good question. I do, but only if I have an adequate habitat for them. If not, we can look them over and release them. We don't want to remove them from an outdoor space that gives them what they need. And, as much fun as it would be, we are not a zoo or a pet shop. We can't house too many. Can you imagine if we had more of them than us? There would be no room to learn."

"Cool. That would be awesome," Phil said.

"Not so awesome if you don't learn enough and graduate. It wouldn't be very fun having to repeat the fifth grade when all your friends move on. That means you would have to be with the fourth graders next year when they move up," Mrs. Webber said.

"*NOOOOOO!*" Phil said, widening his eyes. "My sister is in fourth grade."

Mrs. Webber shook her head at him and then walked back to the front of the room. She whistled, grabbing our attention, and then had us go back to our desks to sit quietly in our seats while she started the projector.

"I want to try something fun. I'm going to blast facts and images at you on the board. All these facts have something to do with me. They are going to come fast, and they are going to be mixed up and jumbled together. You must pay close attention. Then, I'm going to give you a questionnaire and I want to see what you guys learned about me, who was paying attention, and what you picked up over everything else. This isn't a grade. Then, at parent meet and greet, I'm going to test your parents as well."

"HA! I can't wait to see what my dad gets. He will probably get all of them wrong!" yelled Phil.

Phil and Landon started laughing at the idea of their parents flunking the questionnaire. Mrs. Webber snapped her fingers as she went by him, walking backwards up to the front of the room, keeping his eye contact so he would realize to pay attention. With my desk all the way in the back, it was hard to see the board with everyone in front of me. Amanda was sitting on her knees, so I couldn't see over her head.

"Amanda, sit down," I said.

She turned towards me and gave me an annoyed smirk. "No, I don't have to."

"I can't see," I snipped back at her.

She sighed and then sat down on her butt. She turned around and rolled her eyes at me, making a nasty face. Now that she was mad at me, I was probably in the clear of having any more conversations with her.

The words and images started flashing so fast on the screen it was like the beat of a fast pop song. I was trying to remember everything, but it was hard. The only things that stuck in my brain were the images of the Chicago Bears and something about a cat. There was a word up there, but I didn't know what it meant. It said "botanist". I had never heard of it before. It was a short twenty-second PowerPoint presentation. The lights went on and a silly, overjoyed Mrs. Webber came around to each of our desks and placed down a piece of white paper.

"Let's see who knows the most about me now." She chuckled.

Bobby raised his hand. "I saw everything. This is going to be so easy."

"Bobby, keep it to yourself for now," she said sternly. "I'm going to read the questions and then we will go through them.

First question: How many pets do I have?

Second question: Am I married?

Third question: What is a hobby of mine?

Fourth question: What is my favorite sports team?

Fifth question: How many years have I been teaching?

Sixth question: Where was I born?

Seventh question: What is my first name?

I will set the timer. On your mark, get set, *Go!*" Mrs. Webber yelled.

We finished writing at the ten-minute buzzer and then we put our pencils down. I had at least three correct, but I was stumped on the rest. She came around and picked up each paper.

"I will take these. Let's go over them out loud. Who knows what pet I have?" Mrs. Webber asked.

Phil raised his hand. "You have two, one cat and a hamster."

I bonked myself in the forehead for missing the hamster. I was surprised for an animal lover that she only had two pets. I guessed and put down four.

"Jayden, do you think I am married by what was shown on the board?" she asked.

Jayden looked up at her and scrunched his nose. "Umm...yes," he said unsurely.

"Okay, why do you think that?" she asked.

"There was a picture of a ring," he said, in a slightly questioning tone.

"Yes. You are right. Mr. Webber and I have been married for five years. We have no children and we have two pets. Good. You guys are really paying attention," she said.

I knew when she looked over my paper she would be disappointed because I got both wrong so far. I didn't put two and two together with the ring and being married. I just figured there were no pictures of her husband, so she must not have one. It wasn't a diamond ring. It was just a silver band. *How am I supposed to know?*

"Before I go to the next question, just for fun, can anyone guess what my pets' names are?" Mrs. Webber asked.

Amanda started waving her arms in the air, back and forth.

"Yes, Amanda…" Mrs. Webber said.

"On the video your cat was white and big. I think his name is Snowy."

"Nice try. That would be a good name, wouldn't it? His name is Mr. Miagi, named after one of my favorite characters in a movie called *Karate Kid*. Have you ever heard of it?

"I think my Dad has watched it before," Phil said.

"Why did you name him that? Snowy would have been so much better," Amanda insisted.

"His white hair and the way he plays with his paws, he's like a ninja." Mrs. Webber laughed.

"That makes sense I guess," Amanda grumbled.

"I should have named him after a character on Ninjago. Then, you would have guessed it," Mrs. Webber said, smiling wide.

The class erupted in laughter, yelling out names from the Lego series.

"Yeah, Master Wu or Zane," said Aiden.

"Or, Sushi Chef or Misako," said Carlos.

"Maybe I need to get another cat, just so you can help me name it. I'm sure Mr. Miagi would love another playmate. Then, they can show each other their ninja moves," Mrs. Webber playfully suggested.

Amanda was tired of the ninja talk so she butted in, to change topic. "What about your hamster, Mrs. Webber? I bet his name is Chubby. He was so cute and round like a little ball of fur."

"No, his name isn't Chubby, it's even better. His name is Hammy." Mrs. Webber started chuckling as she saw our faces and grins. "Mr. Webber and I couldn't think of a good enough name. Every time I talked to him I would say that as a joke and it stuck."

"I like that. Can you bring him in one day?" Amanda asked.

"Hmmm...I'm sure I could arrange that. I will see what I can do. Alright, let's get back to our questionnaire. What is a hobby of mine? Any guesses are good. How about it Frankie, what do you think?" Mrs. Webber asked, winking at me.

Why did she have to ask me about this one? I knew the next one was the Chicago Bears. I remembered that weird word, but I didn't want to embarrass myself in case it was related to something completely different. I didn't have any other answer, so I went with it.

"Botanist," I winced.

"Wow! Yes! Great job, Frankie. That's probably a word most of you haven't heard. I am a botanist, which is a title for a plant scientist. I have a huge greenhouse in my yard that you would be amazed at. I would love for each one of you to see it before the year's end. Botany includes: algae, fungi, lichens, mosses, ferns, conifers, and flowering plants. I will try and teach you about my hobby as we get to know each other more. We will even try our hand at planting seeds and growing some things of our own. So far, you know I love plants, insects, and outdoors. You are going to be science superstars before you enter the middle school."

I could tell Mrs. Webber was passionate about science. It wasn't my favorite subject, so to say I wasn't completely excited hearing we would have an extra emphasis on it this year, was an understatement.

"Frankie, while I have you on the hook, I know you know the answer to the next question. I told you this morning. Do you know my favorite sports team?"

Mrs. Webber pulled an orange and blue jersey out from her top drawer and held it up in front of her.

I smiled wide. "The Chicago Bears. Same as mine."

"That is right. The Chicago Bears. I spent every Sunday when I was little watching football with my grandpa and my father; we even had season passes. I am a true die-hard fan. Anyone else like the Bears?" she asked.

Many hands went up. I waved mine back and forth excitedly to show my enthusiasm over them.

Bobby continued with his banter about how the Green Bay Packers were better. I ignored him. Phil started calling him a cheese head and Bobby loved it. He started shaking his head and chanting. "Yes! I'm a cheese head!"

The class started to get a little wild talking about their favorite teams.

"Mrs. Webber, girls don't normally watch football," Kristin blurted out, annoyed.

"I disagree, Kristin. I know many that like it. It's no different than softball, soccer, or volleyball. It just depends on what you like. Girls can like any sport, just like boys; What is your favorite sport?" Mrs. Webber asked, looking at her, interested.

Kristin got all jumpy and a smile burst across her face. "Gymnastics."

Bobby interrupted her moment. "My sister is really good. She gets medals all the time. She is the best at the balance beam. No one can beat her."

Mrs. Webber raised her eyebrow at Bobby for speaking out of turn. "Yep, we all have our favorites. Good. I'm looking forward to hearing all about it throughout our time in here. Bobby, next time, let's let our friends talk and not interrupt. And since you said you knew all the answers, why don't you finish up and give me the last three. We are running out of time."

Bobby got a confident and overzealous grin on his face. "Your name is Joanie, you have been teaching for six years, and you were born in Texas."

Bobby started singing lyrics from the song *Deep in the Heart of Texas* with a country twang to his voice.

"The stars at night, are big and bright,

deep in the heart of Texas.

the prairie sky, is wide and high,

 deep in the heart of Texas."

Bobby clapped his hands and shook his body side to side, to make it more dramatic.

Mrs. Webber started laughing. "That explains my love of good barbecue, but unfortunately that is incorrect. However, you are one good singer. Going back to the question at hand, my name is Joanie Webber, but most people call me Joan or Jo and sometimes if they mispronounce it, it's Joanne. I am from Florida, but I moved to Illinois when I was five, so I have been here most of my life. I do wish I still had that sunny weather though. On the video it showed a map and it had an arrow pointing south, that's probably why you guessed Texas. If you would have had more time, I am sure you would have noticed the circle around Jacksonville. I am really impressed Bobby. You almost had them all right."

Bobby furrowed his brows and put his head down. He was mad that he missed one. He was starting to sulk.

"Everyone, get your stuff together. You must go to Art, and then you are going straight to recess and lunch. Fifth grade has the earliest lunch hour and you have recess beforehand this year. When you get back, you have a few worksheets to fill out about yourselves. Put them in the blue turn in bin on top of the filing cabinet in the front of the room and silent read. Make sure you leave the book you want to read out on the top of your desk, so you are not searching for it later. If you don't have one, pick one from the library in the corner," Mrs. Webber instructed.

"We have a few minutes until we need to go. Can we play a short game?" Grace asked.

Mrs. Webber thought about it for a moment. "Sure, but we probably won't be able to finish. We can play a short game of silent ball if you are all sitting quietly."

In the last three minutes, it came down between Austin, Martin, and I. We didn't have time to finish and I was frustrated. Mrs. Webber told us to stop. I knew I would win if we had more time. I wanted to keep going.

"Please, please, please can we finish real fast?" I asked Mrs. Webber, putting my hands together like I was praying.

"No. Let's go, Frankie. We can finish the game tomorrow. Or, if we have enough time, maybe we can do it later in the day. Jenna, please turn off the lights and close the door after everyone gets out. Thank you." Mrs. Webber pronounced.

I rolled my eyes and sighed. Slumped over, I walked to the back of the line and rested against the wall, waiting for everyone to move forward.

"It's just a silly game, Frankie. Why do you get so upset?" Amanda asked.

I'm already annoyed with you. Just give me a minute alone. Please turn around and stop staring at me.

"I'm fine." I widened my eyes at her, sticking my head out and shaking it, letting her know I didn't want to talk.

Why is she even talking to me? I thought she was mad at me?

Mrs. Webber walked us to the Art room. "Be good, be creative, and have fun."

Then, she turned towards me and patted my shoulder. "Frankie, can I talk to you real fast?"

Uh-oh. "Sure," I said.

Mrs. Webber let the rest of the kids go in and she shut the door behind us as we stood in the hallway.

"Frankie, I would like you to set the tone in the classroom. You can be a leader. You have to be a good sport."

Feeling sad that I disappointed her, I looked down. "I know. I'm just competitive."

"Look here, Frankie. It's good to be competitive. I'm just telling you what I see, starting off the school year. I believe in you. I know you can control it. The best athletes know when and where to use their competitiveness," she said.

I shook my head at her, knowing what she meant. Mrs. Webber opened the door and led me into the art room. "See you in a bit," she said. Then, she waved and walked out.

Mrs. Arnold stared at all of us as we got situated at the art tables. She had a wild style, with bright colors of purple, pink, light orange, and yellow on her shirt, a feather headpiece in her hair, sharp rectangular patterns on her pants, and bright purple streaks at the ends of her ponytail. It was hard to concentrate on what she was saying, I was so amused by her outfit.

"Welcome. I am so excited to see you all. I hope you had a good summer. Today, we are not going to dive into anything with our hands, just yet. Last year, if you remember, we learned a little about Vincent van Gogh. I have a video I want to play for you. Pay close attention to the details. Then, I want you to peek at the paintings I have posted on the chalkboard. This lesson is all about self-portrait. Vincent van Gogh painted over thirty self-portraits between the years of 1886-1889. So, he is a great artist to study. I thought this would be a good jumping off point from what we did last year, starting our new lesson.

"Do we really have to?" Bobby asked gruffly.

Mrs. Arnold ignored his comment and kept talking.

"I want you to focus on shading. Look at the lines of the face, the different colors, the background, shapes, expressions, and so on. We will be drawing our own self-portraits and they will be hung in the hallway and featured at the art show later in the year. I have a list of websites that we will use for research, showing videos on how to create symmetry and detecting the correct placement of features. The video is about twenty minutes long. Then, I will come around and take your picture. Next class, I will give you the picture to keep in your folder and you will use it for reference when you are sketching out your rough draft."

Just the sound of this project made me feel exhausted and depressed. *Pictures are the worst.* And drawing myself sounded horrible. *I wish I could trace it, I'm good at that.* We began watching the video and listened to details about Vincent van Gogh. My favorite drawing of his was *Starry Night*. I like all the swirly brushstrokes he used. Some of the self-portraits were a bit different that I was used to seeing, especially the one with a bandaged ear. *Why would anyone cut off their own ear?* Thinking about it, I put my hand upon my own ear, and thought about how badly that would hurt. As the video came to an end, I was trying to concentrate but I kept drifting off, thinking about my football game that was coming up. I was tired. *How am I going to run laps and tackle people at practice tonight when I already have a headache?* I wanted to at least get a touchdown and a pick six in front of Coach, so he would start me. There are only two more practices before opening day. Jayden might be the best quarterback in our league, but I'm one of the best running backs, and together, we are usually unstoppable.

"Frankie?" Mrs. Arnold called out.

"Huh?" I asked, snapping myself out of it.

"I asked you what you noticed in *Self-portrait with Straw Hat*, 1888, summer, post impressionism period, where he used oil and canvas?"

"Oh, uh…"

"Were you paying attention?" she asked.

"Yeah. I just don't remember that one," I said shyly. "They all look similar to me."

"Make sure you are following along," she said, tilting her head at me. "Did anyone else notice the picture I speak of?"

Jenna raised her hand, "That's the one with the pipe in his mouth and he is wearing a hat. It was yellow and teal I think, right?"

"Yes. Very good. What did you notice about the brush strokes?" Mrs. Arnold asked.

"He used different colors to highlight and in his beard, there are thicker marks."

"Great. Yes. If you notice, he did a great job capturing light and shadow. The different shades accent specific parts of his face and the beard is so distinct because of the thicker, heavier brush strokes."

Mrs. Arnold turned on the light and then stood in front of us. "Stay in your seats. I will come around and take your pictures."

I sat in discomfort, dreading the moment she came over to me. "Smile," Mrs. Arnold said.

"Do I have to? Can I do a self-portrait without showing my teeth?" I asked.

"Oh…sure." She snapped a photo of me and then finished up with the last four people.

Noticing it was time to leave, I sat on my foot, getting myself ready so I could get a good head start to recess. Mrs. Arnold dismissed table by table. I ran up to Jayden, sneaking my way in front.

"That was fun," Jayden said, making googly eyes and laughing.

I laughed back with sarcasm, "Oh yeah…."

"So, you want to throw the ball around at recess?" Jayden asked.

"Yeah. Let's see who wants to play," I answered.

Mrs. Arnold opened the door and dismissed us. We walked down the hallway and found the exit door to the playground. Out at recess, on the blacktop, I grabbed a football from the rack and started throwing it around with Jayden.

"Go long!" I yelled.

Jayden turned and went running into the grass, looking back to catch the ball, jumping in mid-air and landing on his side.

"Are you okay? You really caught some air," I shouted. Jumping up and down, putting my hand up to my mouth, I waited anxiously to hear from him.

"I'm fine!" Jayden yelled. He started laughing and got up. "I will throw it to you now. You go."

We threw the ball back and forth. Our friends Micah, Steven, and Sebastian from Mrs. Shubby's class joined us and we started a scrimmage game. They wouldn't let us be on the same team. They said it would be unfair. I didn't like that most of our recess time ended in fights with everyone complaining. Somehow, it was always mine or Jayden's fault if they were losing.

After twenty minutes, the whistle blew.

"We won!" I boasted.

The other team rolled their eyes at me, huffed and puffed, throwing the ball to the ground, except for Jayden. He started laughing and picked up the ball to return it to the sports bin.

"Tomorrow, we will get you back," Jayden said, pointing at me in a funny manner.

Our PE teacher, Mr. Zimmerman, was standing by the doorway, letting classes go in.

"Hey, boys. Nice work on that field. It's a good workout. I expect to see you just as focused at practice tonight. Make sure you are staying hydrated and eat a good lunch."

"Yes, Coach Z," Jayden answered respectfully.

I shook my head that I understood. Mr. Zimmerman was our athletic director, PE & health teacher, and football coach. He was passionate and intense about football. His favorite team was Notre Dame and he was always supporting them with a jersey, t-shirt, or hat, mocking anyone that didn't like them. He attended back in 1982 and his son currently attends, playing on a scholarship. Between the two of them, his obsession was a constant conversation. We liked to rile him up, teasing him.

"Did you see Duke last night, Mr. Z?" Jayden asked him.

"Nah, I had a meeting last night and I didn't get to watch anything. But I heard about it," he answered back.

I butted in. "Yeah, coach you should have seen it. They were up and then Miami did an eight-lateral touchdown, winning the game in the final play. It shouldn't have even counted. It was crazy. Fans were going nuts."

"I should have watched it. I will have to check the highlights when I get home and look at it closely. All right boys, go on in. Grab your lunches and I will see you later," Mr. Zimmerman said.

"Later Mr. Z," I said back.

Jayden and I walked the halls and found our way to the lunchroom.

"I have Doritos today, what do you have? I will switch with you if you have something good," I proposed.

"I have Cheetos. You can have them," Jayden said kindly.

We sat down at a table next to the other boys.

"Anyone want my string cheese?" Jayden asked, holding it up for all to see.

Brian, from Mrs. Shubby's class, stood up and grabbed it.

"I'll trade you my orange juice for your lemonade," Brian suggested.

Jayden looked at his juice box and shook his head no. "Nah…I had orange juice for breakfast. But if anyone has an extra Gatorade, I'll trade."

We looked around, but no one was taking the deal.

"Looks like you are drinking lemonade today," I said to Jayden.

Then, Teddy walked over and put his hot lunch tray on the table next to Jayden and sat down.

"What did you do at recess? I didn't see you," Jayden asked Teddy.

"I just hung out on the swing set," Teddy answered.

"You could have played football," Jayden suggested.

"I didn't feel like playing," Teddy said glumly.

"Okay. But you are welcome to if you want to. We play every day," Jayden insisted.

I could tell Teddy was feeling down. He was upset about something. He wasn't talking much, and he wouldn't make eye contact. We finished eating and headed to line up to go back to class. I pulled Jayden to the side.

"Is your cousin okay? He seems mad or sad or something…"

"I don't know. He probably doesn't like that I'm off doing stuff with you. He doesn't know anyone. I'm sure he misses his friends and stuff," Jayden raised the side of his mouth and shrugged his shoulders.

I felt bad. I didn't want him to feel left out. Heading back to class, Ben kept screaming, making annoying screeching sounds and trying to trip people with his sweatshirt. He thought he was so funny. He tried to do it to Teddy. *Maybe that is why Teddy doesn't seem happy? Maybe he is getting picked on?*

I stepped in front of Teddy, blocking him. "Knock it off, Ben. Leave him alone!" I yelled.

Ben gave me an annoyed face, but he stopped. Then, he went really close to Teddy and whispered something, before going to Mrs. Shubby's room. Teddy stood still with an uneasy look. Ben knew I was serious and that I wouldn't back down, so he instantly backed away. But I couldn't help to think…*if I wasn't there, would Teddy stick up for himself? What would have happened next?* Teddy looked at me and gave me a slight smile, thankful that I came to his defense. Someone had to stick up for him. Ben was in one of his obnoxious moods, where he was unable to control himself and I knew he would antagonize and belittle Teddy for as long as he could. Ben always wanted attention, so he would do all sorts of stuff to get it, even if it got him in trouble. Teddy was the new kid, so he was an easy target.

I had a guilty conscience, thinking about my thoughts earlier about sharing the bus seat. I felt bad for thinking such a way, and not thinking of Teddy's feelings and how he must feel lonely and lost, being in a new school. Before we went back to class, I turned toward Teddy.

"I know Ben said something to you. It's not the first time today, is it?" I asked.

Teddy froze.

"It's okay. Just tell me, please. You shouldn't have to worry about him or anyone else. I'm sorry we didn't watch out for you at recess. You don't have to tell me what he said, just know that I will defend you if you want. Don't feel bad telling the teacher or sticking up for yourself. Ben picks on everyone. He won't pick on me, because he knows I won't tolerate it. Don't let him know it's bothering you. Next time, tell him to back off," I said.

I knew it was easier said than done. I could tell by the way Teddy looked at me, that he didn't want to have any drama or fights. He was shy. Teddy shook his head at me and then walked towards Mrs. Webber's room.

Mrs. Webber was waiting for us in the classroom. She pointed at the white board, so we knew what to work on.

- *Silent Read.*

- *Finish your introduction packet if you haven't done so already. Add one thing to your paper that you want me to know about you. Write one goal for the year. Turn it in.*

- *Add one word to the easel in the back of the classroom. Something that describes your dream teacher.*

- *If you finish, you can go on your computer.*

Reading my new book about Michael Jordan, I looked up and noticed Mrs. Webber. She was wincing and holding her stomach.

"Are you okay, Mrs. Webber?" I asked.

"Yeah, I don't think my lunch settled well. I have a little stomach ache. That's all. No worries. I will be fine. I always get sick at the beginning of the school year. I have the worst luck with that," she answered.

"Me too. I had an ear infection last weekend. It was awful," said Grace.

"Sorry about that, Grace. Glad you are better." Mrs. Webber sat down slowly in her chair. "You have fifteen minutes before we start a new subject. Try and focus."

Looking at the list, I checked each one off, knowing I finished everything. Grabbing my Chromebook, I went into a word document to finish my fantasy football draft with Jayden. I knew he was picking Aaron Rodgers and Odell Beckham Jr., so I typed out Leveon Bell and Antonio Brown. Thinking about my next pick, I thought about my football cards and if I was missing anyone good.

Mrs. Webber's voice interrupted me. "It looks like all of you are done, so we are going to get started. Eyes up here. Please put your computers away."

Oh, man. I wanted to stay on my computer. The computer automatically saved my changes, so I closed it up and slipped it back inside its carrying case. Then, I looked to see what Mrs. Webber was setting up.

"In math this year, we are going to work with decimals and rounding numbers. We will get to that tomorrow. Instead of starting off with a lesson on the first day, I thought we could have a little fun, using our brains. We are going to separate into groups and try and work together as teams. One station will have forty-eight plastic mini cups and you need to build the tallest tower you can in twenty minutes. It's called a stem challenge. Don't forget that you need a strong base. If it falls, you need to start over. Then, in station two, you will have ten minutes to hold up as many marshmallows off the ground as you can, building a structure with toothpicks. You will get points for your creativity. Take your time and come up with a plan. Think of all the different shapes you can build. You get points for design, building structure, and how many marshmallows you use. Listen to each other's ideas. The more creative you get, the more points."

After we separated into groups and sorted our materials on the floor, we started throwing out ideas.

"I've done this before. All we have to do is stack the cups in opposite directions and keep making it taller," said Austin.

"No, it will fall. She said it needs a strong base. I think we need to make it bigger at the bottom. Stacking it in rows and then adding to it, making it skinnier as it goes up in the middle. I saw someone do it on YouTube before," said Mackenna.

"We can try it. If they did it on YouTube, it has to work," Landon claimed.

"Let me know when you have a plan set," said Mrs. Webber.

"We do. We are good," Mackenna said excitedly.

"Okay. I'm going to set this timer. When I say the word take-off, you may begin."

We all stared at Mrs. Webber as she jokingly acted like she was going to press the button on the timer. "Take-OOOO"

Two people grabbed cups, but she hadn't said the whole word yet. She stopped suddenly.

"Boys… start over. Put those cups back," Mrs. Webber instructed.

They grinned and then placed the cups back in their original position.

"TAKE-OFF!" Mrs. Webber yelled, quickly and loudly, leaving everyone in a fluster, not expecting her to say it so soon after telling the boys to put the cups back. Everyone was rushing and talking fast.

"Hold on. Slow down. You are going to tip it and make it fall. Go slow," Austin cautioned.

"Oh no, this doesn't look good. I don't think we made the base strong enough," I worried.

We took it back down and started over. We set out three rows on the bottom and then placed two rows on top of that. Stacking higher, making sure it was balanced, we added cup by cup until it was as tall as us. It started to get tipsy, shaking side to side, and it was just about to fall over.

"Oh, no, oh, no, oh, no!" Landon screeched.

It went down and scattered everywhere, seconds before the timer went off. Putting our hands on our heads, irritated that we were so close, we moved to the side to watch the next round.

"Next group," Mrs. Webber called out. "TAKE-OFF!" she yelled.

They huddled together and started stacking the bottom just like we did, but they were using a method where they would turn the cups opposite of each other, then upside down to stack them, keeping them intact.

A tower had grown, and it wasn't moving. It was getting taller and stronger with each cup. We knew they were going to win.

Mrs. Webber started chanting as the seconds wound down. "5-4-3-2-1...STOP!" she yelled excitedly. Her mouth fell open. "*Wow*. This is awesome. Look at the good work you did. I'm so proud of both teams."

"Yeah, but we didn't win," Landon complained.

"That's not what is important. Working together and watching what works and what doesn't is how we learn," Mrs. Webber explained.

"Next game. Who wants to go first on building the marshmallow toothpick structure? Which group?" Mrs. Webber asked, scanning our faces.

Nobody wanted to volunteer.

"Why don't we continue with the team that just went. You can go first this time."

"Awe, I don't want to go first. Then, they get to see what we do wrong and plan a better strategy, it's unfair," said Kristin.

"You know what, you are right. Let's do it at the same time so we don't have that problem." Mrs. Webber winked at her.

It took us a good ten minutes to draw out practice diagrams. We weren't sure what was going to work. We thought about a pyramid, but we wanted to make sure it could continuously build upward.

"What if we start building a shape with four points, like a square base, laying the toothpicks flat, going into the marshmallows. The marshmallows would be the four corners. And we can build upwards from there. To create length, we then stick toothpicks in the top of the marshmallows and hold them upright into another four marshmallows. We could build multiple towers at the same time and then connect them all together into a rectangle at the end," I suggested.

"Hmm...that sounds good," Grace agreed.

"Yeah, I'm good with that. Let's try it," Carlos perked up.

I shook my head yes. "Landon, Austin, and Mackenna, are you good with that?"

"Yep," they said.

Mrs. Webber placed the timer on the desk and everyone started sorting supplies. "Don't rush, I want you to take your time. I'm not going to use the timer for this one, but I will tell you when to stop. Go ahead and begin."

Working together, we began building multiple towers, so we would have more marshmallows used by the end of our time. A few of us poked our fingers with the toothpicks and smooshed the marshmallows, as we tried to get the toothpicks to stick. Otherwise, we had a pretty good set-up. Three cubes high and four towers across to form a rectangular shape. It was falling a little to the side, but it was standing on its own.

"Class, it is time to end this project. Put your supplies down. In one group, you will see that they built a large rectangular structure using a cube as their base on all four stacks. They connected each stack, creating one large structure. In the second group, they did multiple structures: a pyramid, a prism, a tetrahedron, and a cube. I love the creativity and the versatility of both. It takes a lot to think up each idea. And, it doesn't matter if it's in one big shape, or in all different shapes. It matters how many marshmallows you held up off the ground and the overall creativity process. I'm happy with what you put together and all the great team building," said Mrs. Webber.

"Mrs. Webber, who won?" asked Macayla.

"Team one received fifty points and team two received fifty points. It's a tie. Two totally different concepts but both worked," Mrs. Webber answered cheerfully.

"We have more marshmallows though," said Austin, crinkling his forehead in frustration.

"Yeah, you do. But I gave the other team more points for the amount of shapes they created and their design. So, it evened out," Mrs. Webber said.

"Ohhhh man." Austin sighed. He looked at me and rolled his eyes.

Mrs. Webber put her arm around him and laughed. "I like that you care."

Then, she walked over to the classroom door and pointed up to the clock. "If you can believe it, we only have study hall left today. Since you don't have any homework and we didn't start any new lessons today, you can have the last little bit of time to yourself. You may move about the room, you can go on your Chromebook, you can read…just keep voices low in case anyone needs to concentrate."

I ran up to Jayden. "Do you want to finish our fantasy draft?" I asked.

"Sorry, Teddy just asked me to sit by him and play Prodigy," Jayden said.

"Oh. I'll do that with you guys. I love that game," I said.

Prodigy is a math game that asks you multiple choice questions. If you answer correctly, you can move up and unlock different levels. It is usually a competition, since it shows what level everyone is on in the class. I want to be number one, so I can be the leader. It was feeling like a breeze, as I answered each question correctly. However, it was hard to concentrate, because Teddy wouldn't stop interrupting, asking Jayden and I for the answers. Not wanting to be rude, I helped him, even though I didn't really want to. Yet, it was the first time I saw him smiling since lunch and I liked seeing him warm up to me.

"Guys, we have about two minutes until car riders are released. Come stand by the door if you are getting picked up today. You can leave after the first bell, when they speak over the intercom and dismiss you," Mrs. Webber said.

When the first bell rang, I ran out to my locker and grabbed my stuff, waving at everybody lining up for the bus. My brother was picking me up, so I was released five minutes earlier with the rest of the car riders and after school students. Jayden waved at me.

"See you tonight!" I yelled.

CHAPTER 2: PRACTICE MAKES PERFECT

Walking out of school, I noticed Will. He was waiting in his truck by the curb to take me home.

"Hey, Frankie boy. How was your first day of school? You survived," he said charmingly.

"It was good. How was yours?" I asked.

"We actually did a lot today. I had wood working, chemistry, trigonometry, and creative writing. We got tons of homework. You should be glad you are still in elementary school," Will said.

"Did you have any classes with your friends?" I asked.

"Matt, Scott, Hayden, and Lauren."

"Sean wasn't with you?" I asked.

Sean was Will's very best friend since kindergarten. I was surprised they didn't hang out.

"No, he is doing work study, so he's gone at eleven every day now."

"That's cool. I want to do that." I said.

"Get that sports scholarship and you will have it made brother," Will said with a smirk.

"You should have stayed in lacrosse. You could have done the same," I said.

"Good thing we are so smart. I should get a good academic scholarship," Will said confidently.

Will is a genius. He is ranked number two in the school. He is brilliant. He never has to study for anything, everything comes super easy to him. I'm smart too, but I have to work for it. Knowing Will is leaving soon for college, despite how much we tease one another, I know I will miss him. I don't want him to go far away. He is the best brother and I really look up to him.

"Thanks for picking me up. I wouldn't have had enough time to change and eat before practice if I took the bus home," I said.

"Sure. You owe me. Like…you can do my chores for the week." Will laughed.

"No. that's not fair. Mom would never make me do that," I said, raising my voice.

"I could take you back to school if you want to," Will said sarcastically.

"Knock it off, Will." I leaned over and playfully punched him in the leg.

"Hey! Do that again and you will be sorry." He took the hat off my head and hid it by the door of the driver's seat.

"Give it back! It's my favorite!" I yelled.

"Nope!" Will ignored me and turned up the radio to drown me out.

"Will! *Ugh*," I grunted.

"You started with me. I'm finishing it," Will joked.

Pulling into the driveway at home, I jumped out and went around to the driver's side, looking for my hat. He tried blocking me and then moved swiftly out of the way, so I fell into the truck.

"Ow!" I yelled.

Mom came outside. "Boys, get inside. Frankie, you need to get ready for practice. Ten minutes and we have to leave. If you have homework, please do it now. Get a snack, change, and get your equipment in the car please. Will, are you going to work tonight?"

"Yeah. I will be home at nine. I'm covering someone's shift. Natalie is sick with the flu, so they need another sales associate," Will said.

"I just heard on the news that the stomach flu is going around really bad right now. Wash your hands. Dad will be home in a little bit. Maybe you can hang with him before you leave for your shift," said Mom.

I took my stuff inside and laid it on the counter. Mom and Will followed behind me.

"Guess what, Mom? I don't have any homework. But you do. There's a worksheet to fill out." I was amused that she had something to do and I didn't.

"Homework? I have homework?" Mom started laughing, "Wow. I haven't had homework in years."

I took my folder out and took out the sheet of paper, handing it over to her.

"*Ohhhh*...I have to fill out information on you," she said.

"Yeah, it's easy," I said.

She put her hand upon the top of my head and patted my hair. "I missed you today."

I looked back at her and gave her a smile and a hug. "Is Dad going to pick me up from practice?" I asked.

"Yes. I think so. He will meet you there. He has a meeting after work, but then he will be on his way."

"He worked late last night," I fussed.

"I know. Think of how Dad feels. He is probably really tired. He is working really hard for our family," she reminded me.

"Yes. I know. I just hope he's at my game on Saturday."

"He wouldn't miss it for the world. All of us will be there. How else are we going to yell like crazy and blow the new horn I bought?" Mom joked.

"Oh my gosh, Mom," I griped, while putting my hand over my eyes. *I hope she isn't serious.*

I opened the pantry and grabbed a protein bar and a banana. Then, I rummaged through the fridge and grabbed a string cheese and a water.

"Eat up and put your shoes on. Or, meet me in the car and bring your stuff with," Mom suggested.

She grabbed her purse and went to leave.

"See you later, Will. Have a good night at work. Be safe."

"Mom, do you have my mouth guard?" I asked, yelling after her.

Mom opened the door and yelled back. "It's with your pads and helmet."

I ran to go to the bathroom and then grabbed all my stuff that was sitting in the laundry room. Rushing out, I jumped in the car and slammed the door.

"Let's go," I insisted.

"How was school today?" Mom asked, as she locked the doors and started to drive.

"It was good. I really like Mrs. Webber. She is cool. She likes every sports team that I do, and she is originally from Florida. You know I love Florida. I want to play college football or baseball there."

"I'm so glad to hear that. It makes such a difference when you like your teacher," Mom expressed.

"Today was kind of a free day. We did a lot of games and had a bunch of personal time. It was fun."

"Maybe fifth grade won't be as hard as you thought," Mom said.

"I was thinking that too, but we haven't started anything yet. Math seems like it might get hard. We have a lot of multiplication and division this year."

"You are great at multiplication, so you will be just fine. Just practice your facts."

Mom pulled in to the gravel parking lot, behind the field post of the football field. She turned the key off and got out of the car. Opening the trunk, she picked up my bag of stuff and set it down on the ground.

"Come grab your stuff. I will see you at home in a few hours," Mom instructed.

"Bye, Mom."

Jayden was setting up cones. I took the football and kicked it high in the air, near him, to get his attention. He looked towards me and started laughing. He grabbed the ball and threw it back. I ran over to help him and jumped into the mats that were laying on the ground.

After the whole team arrived, we did our normal running drills, blocking and tackling, and ended in a scrimmage against each other. The night sky was starting to darken, and headlights began to appear one by one, as our parents pulled in to pick us up. Coach Z finished up in a huddle, chanting.

"PLAY FAST, HIT HARD! WHO'S HOUSE IS IT?"

"OUR HOUSE!" We all yelled back.

We jumped around, yelling hu-rah and then broke up our circle, leaving for the night.

Getting in the car, I was looking forward to my bed, but I was disappointed because Dad didn't come. I turned towards Mom.

"Where is Dad? You said he would pick me up," I asked inquisitively.

"He is on his way home right now. You can tell him all about your first day. He got caught up in that meeting. Sorry, buddy."

"Mom, I am so tired," I said.

"Good thing it's late and almost bedtime. Take a shower and then go right to sleep so you get good rest. *Phew*, you smell." Mom looked at me and started laughing, while scrunching up her face.

"*Moooooooom!*"

I laughed and then tried to hug her, wiping my sweat on her. She shrieked and pulled away from me. I couldn't control my laughing, it was too funny to see Mom grossed out.

A few miles later, after listening to Mom sing country music hits, we pulled into our driveway.

"Dad is home!" Mom shouted. "I see his truck in the barn."

"Thank goodness," I said with dramatic tone.

"Okay, funny boy, out of my car." Mom smirked at me, letting me know she was kidding and then kept singing nice and loud, echoing outside.

"The cowbooyyy!" Mom sang with a southern accent, dragging out the words to emphasize the twang in her voice.

I shook my head at her in embarrassment. Even though I couldn't help giggling, she always made me laugh. Mom is always silly. Dad came out of the barn and started to walk up to us.

"Hi, Dad!" I yelled enthusiastically.

Dad ran up to me and tried drilling into me, in tackle form, with his head down, into my waist. Then he started laughing.

"How is my superstar running back?"

"Good," I said.

"Sorry I didn't make it to practice. I want to hear all about it, and maybe you and I can catch the ESPN highlights before bed?" Dad asked suggestively.

"Yeah! Mom wants me to shower first. I will meet you in a few minutes," I said.

"Okay, I will eat dinner then," Dad said.

"*Mmm*, I'm hungry too. Mom, can you make me something?" I pleaded with her, using my full toothed grin and charm.

"Yes. I will make you nachos."

"Yum. I love nachos. Please make it cheesy and spicy," I said.

"I know. From the mouth of Frankie… cheese, cheese, cheese, spicy, spicy, spicy. What would you do if I took away cheese and fattening foods?" Mom joked.

"That would be horrible," I hollered.

"Good thing you eat your fruits and vegetables most of the time," Mom said.

Then, I ran to the bathroom and grabbed a towel, so I could wash up. After my shower, Dad and I sat at the table and shared a plate of Mom's nachos.

"How was your first day, buddy?" Dad asked.

"It was a great first day of school. My teacher is awesome. She is so nice. And I can't wait for my football game on Saturday. Jayden came back from Arizona today."

"I'm so glad to hear that. I will be there on Saturday. Mr. Z asked me to assistant coach."

"Really?" I asked.

"Yep. Are you okay with that? That means I will be there all the time. He really needs help. Mr. Anderson can't do it, so he needs extra hands on defense," Dad said.

"I would love that. Yes."

"Mind if I drive you to school tomorrow? I have a late start for work, so I figured you and I can run through the donut shop and then I can bring you." Dad waited for my response.

"*Yes!*" I answered excitedly.

I rubbed my belly thinking of a chocolate frosted donut and an egg, sausage, cheese, and croissant sandwich. *Yummy*.

"Is Will coming with us?" I asked.

"If he wants to," Dad responded.

"Why don't you ask him yourself, he just came in the door," Mom uttered.

"Hey, hey, hey, Familia," Will said loudly.

William was loud and boisterous and over the top most of the time, completely opposite of me. He was a character, the class clown, a true attention seeker. He always had something witty to say.

"William, how was work? Did you sell a lot of sporting goods? Do you want some nachos?" Dad asked.

"Work was good. I ran through the drive-thru on the way home."

"Dad and I are going to the donut shop before school, do you want to go with us?" I asked.

"No. I'm working on my figure," Will moaned sarcastically. "I actually have to drive Miriam from down the street. Her car broke down. She asked me if I could drive her tomorrow."

"Miriam, huh?" I prodded.

"Don't start," Will snapped back.

Dad and I started laughing and I almost spit out my food. I loved riling Will up.

"I think it's time for bed. I need to go to sleep, so that means you do too," Mom ordered.

"Dad said we could watch the highlights together," I informed.

"Okay, 9:30 at the latest," Mom stated.

Dad grabbed Mom's hand and then smiled at her. "You look pretty."

Mom blushed, said thank you, and then went to her room. Dad and I went and sat on the couch to spend the last fifteen minutes hanging out.

"Dad, do you think I will do good on Saturday?" I asked.

"I do. I think whatever you do, if you are trying 100%, you are going to be great. Just believe in yourself. You need to have confidence. If you want it, you will earn it."

I knew what Dad was saying, but I didn't know how to let my fears go. It was an important game. *What if I mess up? What if I get taken out of the game? What if I get hurt?* It was all weighing on my mind. Yet, I knew what he meant. I was the only one that could control it. I need to stop worrying about everyone else. My eyes were getting droopy and I was exhausted.

"Dad, I'm going to bed."

"Okay. See you in the morning. Dream about donuts," Dad joked.

I went into my room and plopped down onto my bed. The first day of school was a good one. I was looking forward to the next. I just needed sleep. Lots and lots of sleep.

CHAPTER 3: MAGICAL TRICKS AND HULLABALOO

I watched carefully as he jumped around in the dirt and his legs sprang forward. His wrinkled, scrunched up body hopped into the grass to hide. Covering him with my hand, I placed my fingers on top of him to keep him from jumping. *Mrs. Webber will love him.* Running into the garage, I shuffled through my dad's bins.

"Ah-ha!" I shouted.

I knew we had an old shoe box. Placing the frog inside and placing the top back on, I picked up a pencil from the work bench and punched small holes into the cardboard, so he could breathe. I couldn't wait to show Mrs. Webber and add him to the classroom tank. Placing the shoebox into my backpack, I left the top of my bag unzipped, letting it get air. I didn't want to get in trouble from Mrs. Suzanne for having him on the bus, but I wanted to get him to school safely and I knew my parents would say no. I ran inside to stop my dad from getting ready for the donut shop.

"Dad, I want to ride the bus today. I'm just going to eat a granola bar. I will see you after school."

He came out of the bedroom, ready to leave. "Really? You don't want to go? Why?" he asked.

"I'm not hungry. I want to ride with Jayden this morning. He wasn't on the bus yesterday," I said.

"Okay, buddy. See you later. Have a good day."

"You too, Dad."

I reached over and gave him knuckles, trying to refrain from getting too close, so he didn't catch onto my secret. I turned around and dashed out the door into the garage. Picking up a basketball, I threw some hoops until I saw the bus coming. I was determined to be as nonchalant as possible, so no one could tell I was hiding a living creature in my bag. Thoughts of him getting loose and hopping around the bus made me anxious, but the excitement I had made it worth it.

I waited to tell anyone until Teddy and Jayden got on the bus. Scrunched together, us three, it was hard to move around without making a lot of noise. I waited patiently to show them, so the girls in front of us didn't make a big stink about it. If they caught on, they would scream and yell. After picking everyone up and heading down the highway, we were approaching school. It was time to tell them. I couldn't keep it in anymore.

"I have a frog in my backpack," I blurted out in a whispery voice.

Jayden's eyes grew wide. "Whaaat? Cool! Can I see?"

"I'll show you guys when we get off." I pointed at the girls, so they knew why.

"Okay," he said, shaking his head that he understood.

Teddy was untalkative. I wasn't sure how to break him out of his discomfort and get him to open up to me. I thought we had a breakthrough yesterday.

"Teddy if you want to, Jayden and I can play something else at recess today, since you don't want to play football," I said.

Part of me did not want to offer such a thing, but I knew he wanted to hang out with Jayden, and I wanted him to have fun with the both of us. Teddy cocked his head to the side and shrugged his shoulders.

"Like basketball, maybe?" I suggested.

"Sure," Teddy murmured.

Jayden gave me a look, raising the side of his mouth, disinterested in the idea.

"I'm getting tired of fighting with everybody anyway. They can play for a day without us," I said.

Jayden agreed. Teddy started laughing.

"Yeah…it does seem to get crazy. I heard everyone yelling yesterday," Teddy said quietly.

"Then you don't have to worry about Ben bothering you either. With the both of us, he won't come near you," I assured.

Teddy turned his head and looked in the opposite direction. His cheeks were blushed. Jayden squinted and raised an eyebrow at me.

"What are you talking about?" he asked.

I forgot I didn't tell him about it. *Maybe Teddy didn't want Jayden to know?*

"Ben was being silly yesterday and Teddy was in the way."

"Ben is always like that. You just have to ignore him," Jayden said unconcerned.

Teddy rolled his eyes. I could tell he was done with the conversation and that he wasn't pleased about Jayden's lack of compassion. We stepped off the bus and the three of us walked inside together, through the hallways, getting to our lockers. Today, Mrs. Webber wasn't waiting outside to greet us. Peeking over at the door, a man was standing inside the room by the front table. *We never have male teachers, except Mr. Z.* I was kind of excited for that reason, but I was nervous about my box and what he would say about my frog, not knowing me or Mrs. Webber's rules and what we discussed about bringing them in. *Ugh. What do I do? I can't give this to the substitute--he will make me put it outside.*

Trying to avoid his eye contact, I moved to the side and slowly walked with my box on top of my folder, into the room, towards the back.

"What do you have there, sir?" The sub asked, walking in front of me.

"Um...it's something I found for Mrs. Webber. She wanted to see it and said I could bring it in," I said.

"Okay," he said, bouncing around. He was very jolly and a bit different in the way he dressed.

Gosh, I was all worried for nothing.

"I am Mr. Potter," he said, smiling.

"Hi, Mr. Potter. I'm Frankie."

Then, Bobby came up to us.

"Are you related to Harry Potter?" Bobby asked, butting in.

He started to laugh at his joke, but I was irritated. He always found a way to interrupt me.

"No, but I get that one a lot. You are not the first person to ask. That's a popular book series. Wouldn't it be cool if I was? I'm Gerald Potter III. Much better if you ask me," he said, laughing back.

"Mmm…not really. Harry Potter is the bomb diggity. Probably the best books and movies ever. I went to Disney World over the summer and I got to visit Hogwarts. I've got to go back," Bobby said.

Landon made a loud grunt. "*Oh*, man. I thought maybe you had some cool magic up your sleeve. That would make a fun day of school."

Bobby was still going on and on about his *Harry Potter* fantasies. Sometimes, I thought he lived in his own dream world. He always found a way to relate everything back to that series. Teddy got all excited because he loves it too.

"I love *Harry Potter*," Teddy yelled.

Bobby and Teddy made eye contact and became instant friends with that in common, talking about all the characters.

Mr. Potter turned around to entertain their conversation. "I guess you are right. I'm not *that* cool. However, some people think I look a lot like Headmaster Albus Dumbledore, because of my facial hair and coloring, but I think I need a longer beard to pull that off."

"You do have a cool hat," Bobby said. Bobby's mouth was hanging wide open. "And I can't believe you know the characters. Have you read all the books? Who is your favorite?"

"Mr. Potter, you shouldn't have gotten him started," said Jenna.

It was hard for me to follow along because I had never read the series, so I didn't know who they were talking about. With Mr. Potter distracted, it was the perfect moment for me to sneak the frog into the tank. I opened the top of the tank and gently dropped him in when no one was looking. Then, I went to my desk and placed the shoebox underneath. I sat down in my seat and ignored all the ruckus.

"Okay, class. Let's talk about something a little more school based. I'm here today because Mrs. Webber came down with some dreadful stomach virus that has her very sick. We don't want her back here until she is feeling better, right? Otherwise, all of you will get sick too," said Mr. Potter.

"No way. I can't get sick. I have a dance recital on Saturday," said Amanda.

"Yeah. I have a soccer meet in Wisconsin. I can't miss that," said Austin.

"How could Mrs. Webber have a sub already? It's the first week of school. How is that possible? This is the second day. I thought teachers weren't allowed to have subs that early. My aunt said she couldn't take time off yet at her school," Macayla said.

"It was an emergency. She had no choice. She can't physically do her job right now. If she could, she would," Mr. Potter answered.

"I bet she's getting her nails done or something girly. My mom always does that," Carlos blurted out.

"No, I don't think so. Let's get back on track, okay?" Mr. Potter looked at Carlos with raised eyebrows.

Carlos shrugged his shoulders and mumbled something under his breath, but we couldn't hear what he was saying.

"Since yesterday was the first day of school and you didn't have any homework or get into anything, we are actually going to get started on some lessons today. Your teacher is doing something new this year. It's called Genius Hour. You have a partner and you must come up with a project of your choice to create, craft, inform, and generate. Do whatever you think is important to educate us. You will have to put together a 3-D model and present it to the class at the end of the month. You will work on this every week on Fridays, so she wants you to document your classroom time and write a paragraph in your journals about what you did. Write down your supplies and then go home and get them all together to bring them in. Once you have everything set up, you will be able to build it in class. Any questions?

"Can I be with Frankie?" asked Jayden.

"Okay, before everyone goes crazy trying to find a partner, close your eyes and count to 10. Who is the first person that comes to your desk? Go! Beep Bop Badoop!" Mr. Potter yelled out.

What? I don't get it. I'm confused. I peeked and opened my eyes. Everyone was still sitting in their seats. They were just as confused as I was. They must not have understood what he said either.

Mr. Potter chuckled. "That didn't work like I thought it would. Let's try that again. Baboom! To the moon! Go! Get up! Find your partner. You are set free. Spend this hour wisely."

I widened my eyes over his quirky demeanor and over-the-top character. His personality was unexpected. He was kooky and a little different than most subs we were used to. He had a wildness about him. Looking over at him, he was shaking his body all around, making silly faces. His hat was tall, covering part of his white hair, with a little floppy tassel at the end. As he walked around the room, he twirled it around his finger.

Everyone got up out of their seats in an abrupt manner, yelling and running. Jayden and I ran to the corner of the reading center where the bean bag chairs were.

"What do you want to do?" I asked.

"Something with baseball?" Jayden suggested.

"Yes, we can create a baseball diamond and then write about all the historic facts. Which one do we want to write on? The Chicago Cubs?" I asked.

"Or Fenway. I went there two years ago with my dad," Jayden suggested.

"We had a 108-year curse, a historical World Series win, and it's our favorite team. We have got to do the Cubs," I insisted.

"True," Jayden agreed.

Teddy came over and sat next to Jayden.

"What are you doing? What's wrong?" Jayden asked.

"I don't have a partner," Teddy said shyly.

"Oh."

Jayden looked at me and side-mouthed words to me, asking if it would be okay for him to join us.

"I figured you were going to be with Bobby, because I saw you guys talking," Jayden mentioned

"Well, he was already with someone, and I don't know him that well," Teddy answered.

"You can be with us if you want. We are doing something on baseball, are you okay with that?" I asked.

Teddy shrugged his shoulders and scrunched his face. "Whatever."

Mr. Potter was whistling as he walked around the room. It was rather distracting.

"Does anyone else think Mr. Potter is a little strange?" Seraphina asked, leaning over.

I furrowed my brows and watched him for a minute.

"Yeah…he's definitely bizarre," I said.

"Jeremy from Mrs. Shubby's class warned me that we need to be careful with our classroom pets," Seraphina warned.

I scrunched my face.

"Don't look at me like that--That's what he said," she continued.

Mr. Potter was circling around the pets, watching them intently. *Why would Jeremy say that? What would a substitute want with our pets?*

Mr. Potter was very whimsical and goofy. He was juggling chalk sticks and pulling handkerchiefs out of his pockets that never seemed to end. Bobby kept laughing, watching him. I had no idea what to expect from him. *Why is he doing that?* He had an ornate sense of humor and was a bit peculiar, wearing the most unusual outfit that looked like it had been worn many times before. He had a long grayish green overcoat on, that draped and flowed as he walked. It looked soft like velvet or silk. His hat alone seemed odd. I thought he was kind of funny and charming with his jolly nature, but quite a mystery to figure out. *Who wears stuff like that?* Definitely not teachers.

"Mr. Potter, where did you get that hat? Do you wear that a lot?" I asked.

"I have had it for a long time. I wear it when I feel inventive or imaginative or magical. I knew I would be around brilliant kids with all sorts of creativity, so I thought it would be perfect. I have all sorts of hats, and I switch them up, depending on my mood," Mr. Potter answered.

Crinkles formed near the corners of my eyes as I squinted. *Hmmm. Interesting.* I knew I needed to watch him more carefully and keep tabs on him to see what he was up to. *What did he mean by magical?*

"Cool," I said back.

He shook his head at me, tipped his hat, and then walked away.

"That was weird. He is very different," I said to Teddy and Jayden.

Trying to refocus, Jayden, Teddy, and I planned our project. We needed to find something to research if we were going to build Wrigley Field. We agreed to do a search on why ivy grows.

"I have an idea on how to build it," I said excitedly.

"I think I have a big cardboard box at home that I can bring in," Jayden added.

"We can color bricks in the background, make a door that opens, put in a bullpen, add a railing and bleacher seats along the walls, and then add the ivy to the front of it," I suggested.

Teddy was sitting there quiet and disinterested. "That sounds fine," he said.

"What do you want to add to it?" I asked, looking at Teddy.

"I don't care," he said.

"How about you do the inside of the field and the scoreboard and if you want to add a concession or something you can do that?" Jaden suggested.

Teddy smiled. "Okay."

We researched on our computers and wrote down our plan. Thirty minutes later, Mr. Potter started spinning an extra-large pinwheel he had in the front of the room. It contained an array of colors that let off prismatic reflections like a rainbow. When the colors hit the sunlight from the window, the whole room filled with sparkling colors and shadows. I had never seen a pinwheel that big. We were all intrigued and mesmerized, focusing our eyes on it, staring in his direction. It was entrancing and hypnotizing.

"*Whoa!*" the class yelled.

"I don't even have to ring a bell or clap my hands, it seems to have gotten your attention. Save all your work and turn in your ideas so Mrs. Webber can approve them. We are going to move on to science. I have something that you will love. I asked the principal if I could do this with you. We got approval, but you all must wear safety glasses and I am the only one that can be near the chemicals. I need you to stand back and watch carefully," Mr. Potter said.

Mr. Potter put on a lab coat and gloves, handed out safety glasses to everyone, and placed five medium-sized glass bowls on the work table in the back of the room. He took out tiny bottles and told us what each of them were before filling the bowls with them.

"I have five different chemicals. I am going to put one in each bowl. When I light them, you will see, that each one burns a different color. It is called Rainbow Flame. I'm not sure if you know this but astronomers can figure out what distant stars are made of by measuring what type of light the star is giving off. In this science project, you can observe and investigate the colors produced when different chemicals are burned. We have calcium, sodium chloride, copper, potassium, and methanol. Most of these are over-the-counter salts and powders but the last one is just alcohol. We can use sanitizer or rubbing alcohol or an over-the-counter. All of these are ingredients you can find at any grocery store. Now, I want you to stand back. I will use my trusty igniter and light each individually. As it burns, you will start to see the flame change color."

As we watched the flames, we could see them change to the colors of the rainbow: red, orange, yellow, green, and blue. Mr. Potter added one more, to make purple. All of us were amazed and didn't understand how he was able to do that. But, beyond the experiment, I was staring directly at Mr. Potter and I couldn't believe what I was seeing. I rubbed my eyes to make sure I was seeing correctly. The frames of his glasses were spinning in colorful circles of the rainbow, just like his pinwheel and just like the flames. *How is that happening? Was that supposed to happen? Does anyone else notice? Is this supposed to be part of the experiment?* After a few minutes, the flames went out and his glasses were back to normal. I looked around, widening my eyes, freaked out over the entire lesson. It was amazing, but unreal. I felt like I was inside of one of those wacky houses at the carnival where the walls and mirrors distort everything. I couldn't explain what I was witnessing, and I didn't want to say anything to anyone else, just in case it was my eyes playing tricks on me. Everyone sat, in shock, with their mouths open.

"So, what did you think?" Mr. Potter asked. His voice was high and animated.

"What did we just witness?" I asked.

"That was pretty cool, huh? Have you ever had fire in the classroom before? Rainbow, no less? Don't try these at home. This is just for an adult to handle," Mr. Potter instructed.

"Did you see that?" I asked, leaning over by Jayden.

"Yeah…that was awesome."

"I mean, did you see Mr. Potter's glasses?" I asked.

"No. Why? What's wrong?" Jayden asked.

"Nothing," I answered.

Hmmm, maybe It was just my imagination. Thoughts of Mr. Potter being some kind of superhuman plagued me. I walked up to Mr. Potter as he dismissed the class to go back to our desks. My curiosity was getting the best of me and I had to get to the bottom of it.

"Mr. Potter, can I see your glasses?" I asked.

"Hmmm…these are my special experiment glasses. I don't let anyone touch them. What would you like to know about them?" he asked.

Mr. Potter pulled them down and his clear blue eyes looked into mine.

"Oh, never mind. I just thought I saw…"

"What is it you thought you saw?" he asked.

"Never mind," I said, insisting to drop it.

"Okay then," Mr. Potter said, walking away.

I walked past the tank of frogs to check on the one I put in there, and I blinked a few times, trying to remember how many were in there to begin with. *Why are there so many?* It looked like there were a few extra frogs inside, and some of them were mini.

"*Wow*, we have a lot of frogs now. There are tons," I said out loud.

Amanda came walking over to me. "Are you kidding? First Mr. Potter has spinning glasses and now there are tons of new frogs."

"Wait…you saw his glasses spin? I thought it was just me. What was that?" I asked.

"I have no idea, but I feel like I am in a different universe," she said.

Who knew that Amanda and I would be on the same page, agreeing on everything. She was the only one I could talk to about it, since I didn't want to tell anyone else and get made fun of. Maybe what Seraphina said earlier about Mr. Potter was true? Maybe we do have to watch our pets? Mr. Potter started talking and wouldn't stop. He started rambling about anything and everything. He was super smart, talking about space, constellations, the sun, the moon, and the planets. We could not figure out where he was going with his thoughts. He was so into it and the language he was using was too difficult to figure out for a fifth grader. He could tell we were lost, and most of us were starting to fidget out of boredom.

"Mr. Potter, I think it's time to go to specials. We have music today," Grace said.

"Oh golly, look at that, you are right. I am over here going on and on and you have somewhere to be."

He started to chuckle and put his pointer finger up and started spinning it and then pointed it to the door as if he was going to cast a spell with it.

"Line up," he said in a dramatic tone. Then, he started singing a song. "Walk with me to the laboratory, frog and newt and you know the story, we are crafting spells…"

I looked at Amanda with clenched teeth. "Oh boy," I said.

"Mr. Potter, I think I've heard that song on YouTube," Bobby said.

"It's from *Clash of the Clans*, a gaming channel on there. It's "The Wizard Song".

My eyes went big and I jumped, startled at the word. Amanda started laughing and grabbed my arm. "OMG, that's it! He could be a wizard!"

We both started giggling, we didn't know what else to do. Jayden came next to me.

"What are you guys laughing about?" he asked.

"Just the song Mr. Potter is singing. Don't you find him unique and different?" I asked.

"Yeah, he's hilarious and super quirky. I want his hat," Jayden joked.

Teddy came over to me. "Are you guys talking about Mr. Potter?"

"Yeah," I said.

"You know, I went to grab something out of my locker this morning that I forgot in my backpack and he was coming out of the teachers' lounge. I saw something interesting."

"What?" I asked.

"He was talking to himself and pointing a wand at things. At least it looked like a wand. I couldn't see well, because I was too far away, but he was amused with himself. It didn't look like anyone else was with him."

"Teddy, did you see anything during the science experiment?" I asked.

He looked at me and side smiled. "Mmmhmm…"

"You did? Geez…thank goodness. Jayden didn't notice anything. I thought I was seeing things and going crazy."

Teddy stayed by me as we walked into the music room. Mrs. Stevenson brought out our recorders and asked us to find a partner to practice notes. Jayden looked at me, but Teddy was staring at me too.

"Will you be my partner?" Teddy asked.

Stopping a moment to think, I looked back and forth at each of them.

"Sure," I replied.

Teddy did ask me first, I couldn't say no, especially because he was just starting to talk and warm up to me. I pointed to Teddy to let Jayden know. He gave me a gruff look and went to find someone else.

"I have sheets of paper up here with a very simple song on it. I want you to practice with your partner. You can do it together but also try listening to one another and giving tips if someone needs help," Mrs. Stevenson advised.

I looked at Teddy. "You can go first."

Teddy put his fingers on the holes and started playing each note slowly. The whole room filled with blowing breaths and high-pitched octaves, going down in decrescendo, getting softer as the beat of "Hot Cross Buns" came out.

"Your turn," Teddy said, finishing up.

Placing my fingers on the recorder, I began to blow into the mouthpiece, but the sound didn't come out right. I started too fast and had to begin again, as my fingers moved to different holes, losing my grip.

"Sorry," I said.

Teddy giggled.

Beginning again, I did it slow, like Teddy did, listening to each sound, one by one, to make sure I heard the melody.

Mrs. Stevenson walked over to us. "Great job, boys. Keep up the good work."

We could see the shadow of a hat appear behind the glass partition by the door.

"I think I see Mr. Potter," I said.

"I wonder what he's doing?" Teddy asked.

"Probably waiting for us to be done. Maybe he's singing and dancing to our music," I said laughing.

Teddy and I played the harmony together a few times and then it was time to line up. Jayden walked up to us and stood by me in line.

"Ugh, that was so annoying. Teddy got to you first. I had to play with Macayla," he said, rolling his eyes.

"I bet she can play anything, she is in band," I said.

"Yep. She wouldn't stop. She played "Hot Cross Buns", "Twinkle, Twinkle Little Star", "Mary had a Little Lamb", and I don't even know what else, I stopped listening. I barely got through one round by myself."

I started laughing. "Well, you can be with me next time. I messed up going too fast. Teddy was pretty good, so it made me look horrible."

Mrs. Stevenson stood by a large aluminum cabinet in the back.

"I will store your recorders in here. I have 5W on it for your class initials and each recorder case has your name. When you come in next time, come grab it."

"All I can hear is toot, toot, toot...toot, toot, toot, I can't get it out of my head," Austin griped.

"That's music to my ears," Mrs. Stevenson said.

She opened the door and Mr. Potter was standing there doing hand tricks with the kindergartners, who were waiting for us to leave. They were giggling and shrieking at him.

"Mr. Potter, what are you doing?" Amanda asked, standing inside the doorway.

He ushered us into the hallway. "Come on. Come on out. Stand still but follow along. Put your right hand out, directly in front of you, with your thumb facing up. Now, put out your left hand the same way. Flip them upside down so your thumbs are now facing the floor. Take your right hand over your left. Squeeze your hands tight, intertwining your fingers. Lift your pinkies once, and then put your pinkies back down. Now, flip your arms over, without breaking hold and getting locked."

Mr. Potter did it with ease. He had his arms perfectly straight again. He made it look so easy. We were all struggling, trying to keep hold.

"It's a mirror image," he said.

Mr. Potter was getting a kick out of everyone contorting their bodies, twisted up like pretzels. The kindergartners were convinced they were doing it right, but many of them didn't have their arms intertwined correctly. They were getting increasingly noisy in the hallway, disrupting other classrooms. Secretary Sanders came out of the office to check on the commotion. She put her finger up to her mouth, signaling to be quiet.

Ben was coming out of the restroom and noticed us in the hallway. He walked over and tried to do it too. He looked at Teddy and stuck his tongue out.

"Keep it up, dorko…did Mommy pick out your outfit today?"

I glared at Ben. Teddy put his arms down and stopped doing the exercise. Mr. Potter looked over and walked up behind Ben.

"Are you joining us, or do you need to be somewhere? My friends aren't mean to each other, so if you have come here to be anything other than nice, I suggest you head back to class."

Teddy was stiff like a robot. Ben turned on the charm in front of Mr. Potter.

"I love your arm trick, you are super talented."

"Thank you," Mr. Potter said, keeping a straight face, so Ben knew he wasn't going to pull one over on him.

Mrs. Stevenson walked out of the classroom and greeted the kindergartners to enter her class. She waved goodbye to us and winked at Mr. Potter. Mr. Potter apologized for keeping her waiting. He clenched his teeth at us and then started walking us back to class. Getting back to the room, he wanted to know what we thought about his hand trick.

"Well, did you like that? I have many tricks I can show you."

"Mr. Potter, it's going to have to wait. We are supposed to be at recess, we weren't supposed to come back to the classroom," Mackenna said.

"Golly Gee, did I run the time again? Mackenna, please lead the class outside and take the lunch bin. You should have told me. I'm sorry. Be good, have fun," he said.

We fast walked and rushed to get outside, so we didn't miss any more of our free time. Jayden and I went to grab a football.

"Are you guys playing with me today? Don't you remember, you said we could play basketball?" Teddy asked.

I gritted through my teeth and looked over at Jayden. "Oh yeah," I mumbled under my breath.

Jayden looked at me and raised the side of his mouth, slumping his shoulders.

"It's okay. I'll go play on the swing set again," Teddy said.

"No. We will play," I said.

I widened my eyes at Jayden signaling to him that we had to play and couldn't be mean. We put the football back and each grabbed a basketball.

"Want to play shoot out?" I asked.

"Yeah, I like that game," Teddy said.

Teddy was making every basket. Jayden and I were getting frustrated because we couldn't knock him out, but I was really impressed. I had no idea he was so good. He wasn't naturally athletic and usually didn't like to partake in sporting activities. We went shot to shot for five rounds and then he knocked me out. It was between Jayden and Teddy. Jayden wasn't used to losing. Teddy wasn't letting up. He swooshed it, just as the whistle blew and Jayden gave up.

"If only we had more time, I would have won. It's Mr. Potter's fault for keeping us so long after music," Jayden moaned.

I giggled over Jayden's attitude and rolled my eyes, knowing that I often displayed the same. After giving Teddy a high five, I hustled my way to the line to go in for lunch. It was pancakes, sausage, and a hash brown for hot lunch and my mouth was watering thinking about it. Grabbing my tray, I went to sit down.

Mrs. Walters, the lunch monitor, started speaking on the microphone.

"If you have hot lunch, make sure you check underneath your tray and see if you have a red mark. If you do, you are the winner of Lucky Tray Day. You win a prize. Come up at the end of lunch and pick something out of the bucket. We have new pencils, erasers, balls, slime, small books, yo yos, and other little trinkets that were donated by a local parent."

I picked up my tray and looked underneath, letting out a big sigh. "Yes! It's me. I'm the winner. I never win raffles or prizes. I usually have the worst luck."

"Not today. What are you going to pick?" Jayden asked.

"I don't know. Maybe a ball or slime," I considered.

Excitement filled my body. I was so happy to win something. Taking one last bite of my syrup-filled mini pancake, I licked my fingers, threw my stuff in the garbage, and kept my tray to show Mrs. Walters.

Mrs. Walters took my tray and looked underneath.

"All right! Nice! I have a winner! Frankie has won the special prize of the day," she announced over the intercom. "Go ahead and pick something."

Shuffling through an assortment of figurines and tchotchkes, I pushed aside the ones I didn't want. There were many toys that looked like they came from restaurant kid meals. On the bottom, was a small nerf football. Taking it out, I showed Mrs. Walters.

"Can I have this one?" I asked.

"Of course, you get your pick," she said kindly.

I smiled at her and then went back to the table. Everyone was being dismissed to get ready to go back to class and they all kept trying to take my new football.

"Stop!" I yelled, yanking it away from Ben.

"I wonder what we are going to do the rest of the day. The first part of the day was…interesting," Amanda said.

Teddy shook his head at me. "Sure was."

Mr. Potter was sitting down reading, behind the teacher's desk, when we came in.

"Hey guys, perfect timing. I was looking through my books and I found one I want to read to you. Go ahead and sit down in your seats."

Mr. Potter grabbed a stool to sit on. He set it down in the front of the classroom and leaned on it.

"It's called *The Lightning Capturer*."

He showed us the cover of a little boy with a long silver sword in his hand, headed to a city, where lightning was striking above.

"It is one of the first graphic novels I have seen that really pulled my attention. As you get into reading and literature this year, I want you to take notice of all the different kinds of stories out there. And how they are all published and illustrated. It's not always 'one kind fits all'. Look at the details on the page, creating a background, and notice the characters' faces, their emotions and actions are being portrayed so vividly."

As Mr. Potter had us focused in, we could hear "drop, drop, drop" falling from the roof and window. It began coming down forcefully, the longer we sat there and listened to him tell the story. Just as we got to a new scene that was intense, lightning cracked and thunder rolled, leaving all of us jumpy and on edge.

"*Whoa*!" I yelled.

"That sounded like it was close," Amanda said.

"Sure did," Mr. Potter said.

As he finished up the page and bookmarked it, we got up to look out the window. By the time we got over there, the storm had gone through and the sun was shining again. No rain. No thunder. No lightning. Just traces of water droplets on the window sill and grass below.

"That's weird. The storm stopped when you stopped reading the story," Teddy said.

I looked at Amanda and Teddy. Jayden looked at me wondering what we were thinking about. Biting my bottom lip, I whispered into his ear all the things we saw Mr. Potter do. Jayden furrowed his brows and then side-eyed me, not knowing if he should go along with it. He didn't say anything. He may have thought we were crazy, yet he remained unaffected.

"I mean…he was reading a book about lightning and it started to thunder and lightning, maybe he was using…*sorcery*," Amanda whispered to me.

"I never thought sorcery existed. Now I'm starting to question it. I guess it's no different than Santa or the Tooth Fairy or the Easter bunny. We have no real explanation for their magic," I said.

"That's different, he is just a substitute teacher, he's not like Santa Claus," Jayden said.

"Well, why can't a substitute teacher be someone important with hidden gifts, talents, and secrets," Seraphina butted in, overhearing our conversation.

"I guess he can, but it just seems unlikely. I guess you would have me believe that all fairy tales are true? And we live with princesses and witches and goblins?" Jayden asked.

"Well, I don't know about all of that, but let's just keep watch on him," I said.

We began to walk back towards our desks and out of the corner of my eye, another classroom pet stood out to me. "Uh-oh!" I yelled.

"What?" Mr. Potter asked.

"First, we got a new cluster of frogs, and now our salamander has no tail." My mouth dropped open, looking at him, missing part of his body.

"*EWWWW*," shrieked Charlotte.

Mr. Potter walked over and examined him. "He will be fine. Salamanders can regenerate their tail. Sometimes their tail breaks off if they feel threatened."

"What would he have to feel threatened about," Bobby asked.

"I'm not sure. Maybe the frogs, maybe its habitat," Mr. Potter suggested.

"Where did the tail disappear to?" I asked.

"I'm not sure about that either," he answered.

I scrunched my nose, thinking about what Amanda told me earlier, that we should watch out for our classroom pets. And now, I was 100% convinced that she was telling the truth. Too many incidents to ignore. It was all starting to seem too real. I had one thought on my mind and it was clear...Mr. Potter MUST be a wizard. He had to have some form of magic ability. It was the only explanation for all the odd things happening. It was cool, thinking that he could really make things happen. *How could I bring it up to him and ask?* I wanted him to create spells and fly on a broomstick and show us how to do things with his sorcery. I wanted to know if there were special wizard schools and others just like him. No wonder he knew so much about Harry Potter when we came in this morning.

Going up to his desk, I was apprehensive on what his response would be and if he would be honest with me. Just then, as I approached him, I noticed in the corner the coolest dark brown wand with intricate carvings on it. *There it is. There's the wizard wand, the magical spell maker*. I wanted to get my hands on it. I was gazing towards it, in some entrancing way, as if it had a spell on me.

"Yes?" Mr. Potter asked, looking up at me, trying to break me of my stare.

"Is that a wand?" I asked.

"Yes, it is," he said, while smirking.

"What can you do with it?" I asked.

"All sorts of things. Magic. Magic. Magic," he said happily.

Is Mr. potter telling me what I think he is? He is admitting to me that he does magic. This was the best day of my life.

"Mr. Potter, can you show us how you use it and what you do with it?" I asked.

"I could. But I don't want to get fired. I quite like this job."

"Mr. Potter, have you ever subbed here before?" I asked.

"I did one day last year, but that was my only time. I enjoy this school. It has a lot of charm. I am subbing at a few different schools in the area. So, I am jumping between all of them right now."

"I think you should be here full-time," I said.

"Thank you very much, Frankie. I would enjoy that. However, I also work part-time at the space museum. Two days a week, I go into the city."

"No way. We are going there for a field trip," I said.

"Then, maybe I will see you," he said.

I went back to my seat and thought about how amazing it was to have a special gift like that.

Mr. Potter started fidgeting with a playing card in the palm of his hand. I turned away and started straightening my things, getting them ready for the end of the day, so I didn't have to do it later.

"Holy guacamole!" Bobby shouted.

I looked back up and focused on Mr. Potter. The card was levitating and floating up off his hand, as he used his other hand as the guide.

"Whoa! Jumping jackrabbits! What is going on in this class?" Landon asked.

"How are you doing that?" Aiden asked in wonder.

"Can I see the card?" Jayden asked, skeptical and confused.

I widened my eyes and stared in shock. Mr. Potter was the most interesting person I had ever met. He was a real, live, in front of me, magical, wizard. There was a card floating in thin air above his hand, with nothing and no one near him.

"Don't mind this little card, I just use this to clear my thoughts and have some fun. I do it all the time. Next, we are going to get our stuff situated on our desks, because we will be going across the hallway to Mrs. Shubby's room to watch a movie. Mrs. Shubby has a sub today too. Supposedly, she has also come down with the same dreadful stomach virus," Mr. Potter said.

Whispers were going around the room. Everyone was bright-eyed and excited over what they saw.

"Class, look up here. I'm putting your weekly spelling words on the board and your group assignments for reading. Mrs. Webber put you in groups of three or four. She said you will not be staying in these groups, it's just a starting point until she does benchmarking and gives you a level. She wants you to read the first two chapters tonight for homework. I have the books that she chose up here. I will put them in a stack on the front desk. You will be filling out a book summary and questionnaire and she will quiz you on it the next time she sees you," Mr. Potter instructed.

"Awe. I don't want to read, and I don't want a quiz," Bobby said, rolling his eyes in annoyance.

"Look how much fun reading can be. You enjoyed *The Lightning Capturer*. If you dive into the writer's world and you embrace the story, you will immerse yourself into something you never knew existed. You can let everything go and be with the character. Pretend you are in the story, in the setting. If you let your imagination take over, you will find reading much more enjoyable," Mr. Potter explained.

"Well, that's because he's a wizard and his stories actually come to life," Amanda whispered to me, referring to the rain storm that occurred earlier.

I smiled at her, acknowledging her comment. "True."

"I don't have time to read. I have sports after school," Jayden said out loud.

"School is just as important as sports, so you need to balance your time. Can you read on the bus? Can you read before bed? Can you read in the car? Bring your book with, wherever you are," Mr. Potter suggested and rhymed.

"I get too distracted," Jayden admitted.

"You probably need it to be quiet to concentrate, huh?" Mr. Potter asked.

"Yes," Jayden answered.

"I tell you what. When you get home, eat a snack, take the first twenty minutes and go in your room and dedicate that time to reading. Then, you will have it finished and you will be free to go to your sports and concentrate. What sport do you need to go to?" Mr. Potter asked.

"Football. I'm always so tired from school and then after football, I am too tired. So, I never know when to do it."

"Reading is the perfect thing to do when you are tired. It calms you and it keeps you busy, but you don't have to move. You can lie down in your bed, filled with your favorite blankets and pillows and do nothing. No physical activity involved at all. Doesn't it sound perfect?" Mr. Potter asked.

Mr. Potter went on and on about how reading is the gateway of learning. I started to drift off again. As Mr. Potter began talking about beds, pillows, and blankets, I was thinking about how good that sounded. I couldn't wait to lay in my bed.

"I'd rather play Xbox and watch tv," Bobby interrupted.

"Yeah, I don't want to read and do math when I get home. I want to go on my phone," Landon said.

"I know, I know…these days, your phone is everything," Mr. Potter laughed. "If you can believe it, I don't have one."

He looked at our faces and was amused with the looks of disgust, thinking of a life with no electronics.

"How do you survive?" Grace asked with dramatic tone, throwing herself down on her desk, acting like she couldn't live anymore after hearing such a thing.

"I don't need it. And I like my brain cells." He made a silly face at us and Seraphina scrunched her nose at him.

"That's because you have magi…"

"What's that Seraphina?" Mr. Potter asked.

"Nothing, I was just talking to myself." Seraphina was thinking about his magic abilities. She turned around and winked at Amanda and me.

"Looks like it is movie time. Let's get in line and head over to the other classroom," Mr. Potter said, changing the subject.

Everyone got up and walked in a single file line to the other fifth grade classroom. They had a male substitute too, which was interesting, since it's such a rarity at our school. As we walked in, their teacher was standing in the front of the room by the whiteboard, trying to get the tv to work.

"G'day Mates. Arvo, I am Mr. Graham. Take a seat on the carpet!" he yelled out excitedly.

What in the world did he just say? Arvo? Mates? Huh? What accent is he talking in? Dumbfounded and confused, we scanned the rest of his class to see their expressions. They were laughing hysterically. Ben was acting like a kangaroo, hopping and yelling. "Arvo! Arvo!"

Mr. Potter looked at Mr. Graham with inquisition.

"Hello, Mr. Graham. I sure do love your accent and your lingo. It is nice to hear something new and different around here. Can I guess where you are from?"

"Yes, please do," Mr. Graham said, humoring him.

"New Zealand or Australia..." Mr. Potter guessed.

"You are correct. Australia. My students have been looking at me funny all day. I must say things a little different than you guys do. There has been a lot of snickering going on in here.

"I hope they are being kind to you," Mr. Potter said loudly, making sure everyone could hear.

"Mrs. Webber took a sickie, I assume?" Mr. Graham asked, looking at Mr. Potter.

"Uh, yes. She has a stomach virus as well. She will be back Monday. It's a good thing they started the school year on a Thursday. She will only miss one day and now she will have the whole weekend to rest up. I received an email from her that she was feeling a little bit better," Mr. Potter answered kindly.

"I hope Mrs. Shubby comes back just the same, I'm snowed under with heaps of chores at home. I'm not sure I will take another job that soon."

Mr. Potter shook his head and giggled. "I know just what you mean."

Meanwhile, everyone kept laughing, listening to the funny things coming out of Mr. Graham's mouth. We didn't understand anything he was saying, but Ben was taking it too far. He was sitting behind Teddy poking at him and laughing. Mr. Potter interrupted and asked Teddy to join him in the corner of the room.

"Teddy, could you come here."

"Uh, oh, what did you do now, Wetty Teddy?" Ben asked.

Some of the other kids in the class joined in the laughter. Teddy looked completely mortified and I was growing angry. I couldn't believe Jayden wasn't saying anything.

Looking at Jayden, I put my hands up in the air. "Really? Tell them to stop!"

Jayden acted like he didn't know what I was talking about and shrugged his shoulders. Then, he got up and went next to Ben.

"Does it make you feel cool to pick on the new kid? Or are you just jealous? I have the same outfit that he's wearing. I heard you were picking on him about it. Do you want to make fun of me too? Go ahead and try it."

Ben was nervous. Jayden was the most confident, strong, athletic, and popular kid in the school. And now that everyone was staring at him, Ben was embarrassed. They weren't laughing at Teddy, they were fixated on Ben.

"Yeah, Ben. Be nice. We like Teddy!" Amanda yelled.

"Just stop picking on everyone. Why do you have to be so mean?" I asked.

Ben was irritated. He rolled his eyes and pulled his knees up to his chin, sitting on the carpet, hiding his face. I didn't want him to feel sad, I wanted him to be kind. I wanted him to think about what he was doing and change.

"Ben, we all like you, we just want you to be nice. How would you like it if we were doing that to you, sitting behind you and flicking you in the ear and prodding you in the head and back?" I asked.

Ben wouldn't answer.

Mr. Graham turned towards the tv after figuring out how to work the controller.

"Eyes up here. I figured it out. No more talking. We are going to watch *Charlotte's Web*. How many of you have seen this already?" he asked.

Most of the class raised their hands.

"We had to read the book in third grade," Claire said.

Claire was in Mrs. Shubby's class and was extremely nice. She was probably the nicest girl in the entire grade, and she was one of my best friends.

"Then, this should be a fun watch," Mr. Graham said, winking at her.

She shrugged her shoulders and smiled. Mr. Potter turned the lights off and went to sit by the teacher's desk, with Teddy following him. I wasn't sure what Mr. Potter was saying to Teddy, but I noticed him take something out of his pocket and hand it to Teddy. Teddy put it in his sweatshirt pocket and smiled with a full-faced grin. Then, he returned to the carpet with a whole new attitude.

Claire leaned over and whispered in my ear. "You should have seen us today. We had no idea what Mr. Graham was talking about. We were lost. He just kept asking us stuff and we didn't understand. I didn't want to make him feel bad, so I just kept acting like I understood. Mrs. Shubby might have to re-teach us on Monday what we went over today."

I smiled. "Like what? What did he say?" I asked.

"I can't remember exactly, but we were celebrating Evelyn's birthday. She brought in treats for the class. He said he was chockers…or something like that…and then he called the treats fairy floss and choccy biccy. We were laughing so hard. It made no sense."

"That must be the terms they use in Australia to describe sweets," I said, side smiling. "He has an accent, but he doesn't have magic."

"What do you mean?" Claire asked.

"Our substitute is a wizard. I will tell you more later, so we don't get in trouble," I said.

Claire shook her head and smiled at me. "Okay. By the way, are you nervous for your game tomorrow?" she asked.

"Yes. I can't stop thinking about it. I just want to do good. We ended last year with the championship, how do we top that?" I asked.

"I don't know. I'm nervous too. I have to do the new routine for half time and the cheer squad is doing a backflip competition," said Claire.

"You will do good," I said kindly.

Mr. Potter whistled to get us to stop talking. I looked in his direction and stopped speaking, afraid of getting in trouble. *Hmmm...what kind of consequence would I get from a wizard? That was an interesting thought.*

After talking with Claire about football, I was starting to get anxious again. Mr. Potter's magic had taken precedence over my worries today. But now, it was back. I started visualizing Coach on the sidelines yelling, while I got sacked at the 50-yard line.

An hour and thirty minutes later, Mr. Potter interrupted my daydreaming as Mr. Graham turned off the tv.

"We got through as much as we could today. It's time to go back to class and finish up before dismissal. Mrs. Webber's class, see me on the carpet in our room."

I got up and waved goodbye to Claire and my other friends in Mrs. Shubby's class.

"Now, I really want to go to sleep," Jayden said, as he walked across the hallway into our room.

"Me too," I said, wiping my eyes to stay awake.

I turned around to wait for Teddy, but I saw him do the most amazing thing. He went up to Ben, said a few words, smiled, and gave him a high five. I was shocked. *Did Mr. Potter tell him to do that?* I waited for him to join the line.

"Hey, what was that all about?" I asked Teddy.

"I used magic. Mr. Potter gave me his wand and I went up to him and told him that I forgave him, and we could be friends."

"He gave you his wand?" I widened my eyes in bewilderment.

"I know. I can't believe it. I'm worried I'm going to lose it or accidentally use it on the wrong thing. I'm not supposed to point it at anything, he just wanted me to have more confidence," Teddy said.

"You are lucky. That's so cool. Do you have to give it back?" I asked.

"Yes."

Teddy and I joined everybody in the classroom. Sitting on the carpet, we waited to hear what Mr. Potter wanted to talk about. He sat on his stool waiting for our silence.

"I want to talk to you really quick. I noticed something while we were in with Mr. Graham. Many of you and some of the kids in the other class were laughing and making fun of the way he speaks. Most of that was just slang, I believe. We use a lot of that language as well, but we are used to it. For instance, when we say something like 'I am feeling blue or that's a piece of cake'. Can you imagine what he must think of some of our words...just as we think of his?

Imagine how hard it is for the person that stands out against the rest, trying to fit in. I want us to be inclusive of everyone, even if they are not what we are used to."

"Kind of like you?" Teddy asked.

"What do you mean by that? A substitute teacher? A uniquely handsome man with a great personality?" Mr. Potter started laughing at his own comment.

"Well, we all know what you are," Teddy continued.

Teddy pulled out the wand and handed it to Mr. Potter.

"A wizard. It's probably scary not knowing what people will think of you and if they will accept you. People probably stare at you, don't they?" Teddy asked.

"A wizard? Huh, I have never been called that before. Well, I am skilled, and I am clever. In a way, I am a wizard.

The class exhaled. Mouths were open, staring at him, waiting for him to explain.

"A real wizard? Are you sure that you are not related to Harry Potter? Is that series real? Are there more of you out there? I knew it, I knew it!" Bobby shouted.

"We had you figured out. Amanda, Teddy, Frankie, and I pieced it all together," Seraphina said.

I widened my eyes at her for throwing my name out there. *How embarrassing.*

"A wizard, by definition, is someone who practices magic. Most of my tricks and silly antics are just that. I am a magician. I spent fifteen years doing stage acts.

Most of what you saw are illusions. I want you to think they are happening, but it's really a trick to the eye," Mr. Potter said convincingly.

"Oh," I said, feeling silly. I put my head down, ashamed that I had thought such a foolish thing. "But why did you give your wand to Teddy? He said it was the magic from the wand that helped him make up with Ben."

"The magic is your belief and what you do with it, and the wand itself is like your safety blanket. When you know you have something with you to help you through an experience, it doesn't seem so scary. Teddy just needed the confidence to speak up. If the wand helped him do that, then it is magical, in a sense."

"I don't know…I don't really understand," Carlos said.

"When I was younger, I started performing tricks with a magic set and I would get made fun of all the time because the other kids didn't understand it. It was different than what they were into. Now everyone wants to do magic," Mr. Potter said.

"So, your wand is magical, or it isn't? I am so confused!" Carlos continued.

"A wand is just a thing. A piece of wood. A prop. It's what you do with it that can be magical. It is your belief in it."

"How do you explain what happened to the classroom pets?" Amanda asked curiously.

"The janitor came in to clean the salamander's tank. He placed him in the frogs' tank during the cleaning. Something must have happened then. All I can think of is that maybe the salamander felt threatened being near the frogs… Otherwise, your guess is as good as mine. But I didn't want to get into it earlier, because I'm not positive that's the reason, and I don't want you all worrying and being sidetracked," Mr. Potter said.

"How do you explain all of the new frogs…how did they just appear out of nowhere?" I wondered.

"I assume one of them must have laid eggs. Did Mrs. Webber not show you or tell you if there were any?" he asked.

"No, and I didn't notice them yesterday," I said.

"Usually, there are little egg-looking dots. Maybe you didn't know what they were? Mrs. Webber probably forgot to tell you. Also, I might be wrong, but I'm assuming someone brought an extra frog in today and added it to the tank"? Mr. Potter asked.

I sat completely still and looked away from him. *Oh my goodness, how did he know that? I am going to be in so much trouble.*

"In the science experiment, your glasses got all swirly in different colors. How and why did that happen?" Teddy asked.

"They are my special glasses. I spent a lot of money on them for them to do neat things like that. They also make it look foggy if I do anything with explosions," Mr. Potter explained.

"But…when you were talking about rain, thunderstorms, clouds, accumulation, and lightning, it started doing exactly that. You were reading the book and it started. Then, when you stopped reading, it ended. How do you explain that?" Seraphina asked.

"It is the weather, I can't control that…it was by coincidence that a microburst blew through the area at that exact moment. Unfortunately, I am not that talented. That is mother nature at its finest," Mr. Potter insisted.

"Was that floating card just a magic trick?" Bobby asked.

"Yes. I created what we call a 'gimmick card' and all you need is clear plastic and glue." Mr. Potter chuckled.

"Can you show us more tricks that you know?" Bobby asked.

"Do you know that one magic trick where you put someone in a box and they disappear?" Austin asked.

"Or the one where you take swords and slice through the box while someone is in there?" Carlos asked.

"I would need a good assistant and I can't perform those acts in a classroom. I do know how to do some simple tricks that we can do right here in the classroom with things we have laying around, if you want me to show you."

Mr. Potter got up and took a spoon off his desk from his lunch bag. "I can bend this spoon. Watch carefully."

Mr. Potter took the thick, solid stainless-steel spoon and bent it without strain. It was effortless, like Superman.

Everyone gasped.

"*HUH*? Wow. You are strong, Mr. Potter," Jayden yelled.

Then, with one motion of his hand, the spoon was back in regular form.

"*Whaaat?* Let me see that. I bet I can do that too," Mackenna said.

94

Mr. Potter gave the spoon to her, so she could try it herself.

"*Ughh. Grrrr.*" She huffed and grunted, trying to get the spoon to bend easily, but it was difficult, and she couldn't muster the ability.

"Tell us how you did it!" yelled Aiden.

"I just moved the handle further to the inside of my hand. It's all about the positioning. I didn't bend the spoon at all. It is a beginner magician's trick."

"How about another one? Something different," Grace said.

Mr. Potter put the spoon down and grabbed another object. Then, he walked back over to us.

"Okay. Look at my calculator. It's blank, right?" Mr. Potter asked.

"Yeah."

"Now, look carefully. I'm going to ask it to talk to me. In order for you to have a conversation you have to enter a private code. Grace, please type in .07734 and say hi.

We all kept our eyes on it. She typed the code and turned the calculator upside down. Then her eyes grew big and she gasped.

"I see it. It says hello. Well, kind of."

Mr. Potter grabbed it and held it in the air…On the screen was the word 'hello,' in numeric form.

"If you didn't know any better, you would have assumed that I did that with magical powers. Each trick plays with your mind and even though there are simple explanations and ways to figure them out, only the magician knows how. That is the fun part."

"One more *please,*" Macayla pleaded.

"Let's see, I can do a quick one with a pencil."

Mr. Potter grabbed a pencil from Aiden's desk. He held it upright, as he held it by the eraser. Suddenly, it looked like it was bending. It looked like rubber and not wood. *How was he doing that?*

"Mr. Potter how is that happening?" Seraphina asked. She picked up a pencil from the desk next to where she was sitting and tried it herself. It didn't look the same. It was stiff.

"When you hold a pencil by the eraser, and you move it just right, at the right speed, it gives you the illusion that the pencil is bending. It comes with a lot of practice," he said.

"That's cool!" Bobby shouted.

"Unfortunately, we are using all of our study hall time and we are just about out of class minutes. Before I dismiss you, let's get back to what we were originally talking about; someone being different and accepting them. Being ourselves is why we are here. How boring would it be if we were all the same person? If we wanted that, we could just have the Earth run by robots," said Mr. Potter.

"Robots! Awesome!" Carlos yelled out.

"This has been a great day, and I love that my magic made you believe I was a superhuman. I wish that were true. Life would be quite interesting. In reality, I am a substitute teacher and a museum tour guide. I'm normal in that sense. I am a little different. I don't worry about fitting in or being someone I'm not so people will accept me. I am who I am. I am myself and I am unique. Not everyone will like me and that's okay. I like my hats, I like doing magic tricks, I like to keep things fun. I don't want learning to be boring. I don't want to be like every other teacher. What good would that do? You need variety. Everyone I have ever found interesting was an individual, doing something they loved, that isn't based on the norm. I say, be your own kind of weird. If you are getting negative attention from someone, because you are different, something about you stands out for them to notice you. That is your strength. We don't have fifteen Frankie's in this classroom. We have fifteen special kids with their own personalities, style, sense of self, and smarts. Be the youest you, you can possibly be. Stand up for yourselves and for each other. If you need a crutch, grab yourself a wand."

Everyone started to laugh.

Mr. Potter continued as the noise died down. "If you need a hobby, I have many magician's books I can recommend. You made my day. Thank you for that. Mrs. Webber will be back Monday. Today, we did a little bit of work, but I believe she will start all your lessons next week. This is where I say farewell to all my Moose Academy friends. If you enjoyed having me today, you should meet my friend, Mrs. Laurie Watussi. She is a substitute in the district that I co-teach with at the middle school. She takes elementary assignments occasionally. She has many unique traits, just like me. She is very popular. I hope you have her one day. This class would be great with her since you have such good imaginations.

"Like what? What can she do?" Bobby asked.

"She's very good at crafts, she can fold origami in less than ten seconds, and she sings multiple octaves above the normal, a pitch and sound often unheard to the human ear, it is so high. Her platinum white hair almost glows in the sunlight. She is one of my very favorite teachers, and human beings for that matter. She has the rosiest of cheeks. She reminds me of a fairy. She is goddess-like; kind of like one of those characters in *Sleeping Beauty*. You know…that princess movie from Disney fairy tale books…"

The girls were shaking their heads and chit chatting about how fun it would be to have a teacher that was like a fairy god-mother. Everyone got up from the carpet and grabbed their things that were sitting on their desks and went out to put them in their backpacks. Car riders were dismissed and the rest of us waited an extra five minutes until the second bell rang to get on the bus. Mr. Potter stood in the front of the room and let us examine his wand. As the loud beep came across the intercom, we all said goodbye and left the classroom chattering about everything we learned and saw.

As I left, I turned back around one more time to catch a glimpse of his peculiar hat, so I wouldn't forget it. He was hard to figure out, but I think what I like most about him, is that Mr. Potter is his own person and is confident. Mr. Potter has no fear. *I could use a little bit of that (thinking about my football game).* He isn't your normal average sub or average person. He is one-of-a-kind. Even though we are not used to someone like him, it was one of the best days I've ever had in elementary school with a substitute. Normally, I dread having a sub. But today changed that. The day flew by and I laughed and sat in awe through most of it. His humor, magic tricks, and jolly, happy attitude made it a special day that we wouldn't forget. Even if he was here for only one day, I would always remember the day we had a sub with crazy glasses, a wizard hat, and fire blowing science projects.

CHAPTER 4: PREPARATION

"Frankie, what are you doing? You have five minutes until we need to leave for football practice!" Mom yelled across the house.

I was in the middle of reading, resting with my squishy, football-shaped pillow, not wanting to be interrupted.

Mom knocked on the door and came in. "Frankie, did you hear me?"

"Yes. I'm reading."

"Did you eat something?" she asked.

"Yes. I had a snack."

"Do you have all of your stuff ready to go?" She asked.

"Yes. It's all right there on the floor. I'm just finishing my homework. I will be out there in one minute," I said.

Mom was pleasantly surprised. "Okay, sweetie. Looks like you have it all figured out."

Mr. Potter was right. I was feeling calm, rested, and clear-headed after reading. I was ready to go to football and have some fun. And I wasn't worried anymore.

A door slammed, and I popped up and jumped out of bed. *It's Dad.* Walking into the kitchen, I saw him sorting through the mail with his back to me.

"Hi, Dad!" I yelled, to get his attention.

Turning around, Dad furrowed his brows and scrunched up his lips. "What? What do you want?" he said sternly, with a mean, gruff look upon his face.

I stood there for a moment wondering if he was serious or not. *Is he in a bad mood?* Then, he got a full-faced smile and started laughing.

"HA. I got you," he said. Dad loved tricking me and loved being sarcastic. "You thought I was serious!" Dad shouted. He walked up to me and gave me a big bear hug. "How are you, Frankie? Did you have a good day at school? Are you ready for practice?"

I looked at him, tilting my head and squinting my eyes, "I totally knew you were kidding."

"No way. You should have seen your face," Dad said.

I smiled at him. "Okay. You are right. Are we going to leave?" I asked.

"Yeah, I'm waiting for you," Dad joked. "And you never answered my question. How was school?"

"MMMM…different. Very, very different," I said.

"What do you mean?" He asked curiously.

"Our substitute was a magician, so he did tricks all day long," I said.

"Wow. You got an education and entertainment. Lucky kid. Okay, get your shoes on, and I'll meet you in the car. I just have to change out of my work clothes real fast," Dad said.

Mom came into the kitchen and handed me my stuff. "Are you ready for that game tomorrow?" she asked.

"Yes. I am so excited," I said. "Hey, where's Will, Mom?"

"He went to Nana's house for me. I made her some soup. She wasn't feeling well. He offered to drop it off for me."

"Aw, I want to see her too," I said with disappointment in my voice.

"If she's feeling better, she should be there tomorrow," Mom said.

Dad came out from his bedroom and looked at me still standing there, without my shoes on.

"C'mon buddy, we have to go. Bring your shoes with and put them on in the car. Grab a water bottle and say bye to Mom."

"Bye, Mom," I said, giving her a sweet smile.

"Run hard. I will see you later," She said.

Mom got back to folding laundry and watching tv. Dad and I chased each other out to the car.

"I beat you!" I yelled, getting to my seat first.

"You cheated!" Dad yelled.

"*No*, I didn't!" I exclaimed.

"HA. I know. I just had to say that. I'm really out of shape." Dad laughed.

"You definitely couldn't be a running back," I said, teasing him.

"I could be the quarterback, how about that?" Dad asked.

"Mmm...I don't know. You do have a good arm, but you are not as good as Jayden," I said.

Dad turned up the radio to ACDC and blared it. Then, he playfully punched me in the arm. "Slug bug!"

"Ow, Dad!" I playfully punched him back. "Next time, tell me we are playing. That's not fair." I goofily made faces at him, crossing my eyes.

We were both laughing and head banging to the music as we pulled into the parking lot at the football field.

"There's Jayden. I'm getting out." I opened the door and ran up to Jayden and Sebastian, who were practicing kicking.

Coach had us finish our running drills and then form into teams, so we could scrimmage and practice our plays. I couldn't seem to catch the ball and every time I had the lead, they would tackle me. *Ugh. I could really use some Mr. Potter magic right now.* Then, something clicked. *That's it. I need to trick them. An illusion.* It's all in the way I hold it. I need a good fake-out. When we huddled together for the next play, I told everyone what I thought. Coach was excited.

"Good thinking, Frankie. We have one play that is kind of like that, but we haven't really executed it yet. I think that is a good plan. If they always see the same people running the ball, they know where to block and who to target. We have to psyche them out."

The next play, Sebastian pretended to pass the ball to me and I ran, acting like I had the ball in my hand, holding it close to my side. All the while, Sebastian still had it and was running clear up the field, while everyone's attention was on me.

"Touchdown!" coach yelled.

We started jumping up and down, pumped up over our play.

"We will definitely incorporate this into tomorrow's game," Coach Z said.

Dad gave me a thumbs-up from the sideline. Coach Z had us do sprints, push-ups, and tackling drills to finish the night. I walked over to where Dad was and squirted my water bottle into my mouth, trying to catch my breath.

"I'm ready to go home," I said.

"Okay, it's going to be an early night. I want you to get some sleep. I'm proud of your effort tonight," Dad said, rubbing his hand across the top of my hair, making it stick up from my sweaty hygiene.

"Thank you," I said back.

I patted my hair back down and took my shoes off, so I could be more comfortable. As I rode home in silence, Dad took a work phone call and I rested my head against the window. My eyes slowly fell shut and my mind went blank. And that is the last thing I remember.

CHAPTER 5: GAME DAY

The crowd was growing, filling up the bleacher stands. The opposing team was practicing. Cheerleading teams lined the sides of the field, working on their jumps and flips. I caught a glimpse of Claire practicing her roundoffs. She noticed me and yelled out my name. I waved at her and smiled. My nerves were bundled up, but they were full of positive energy. Excitement filled me up from the music that was coming from the speaker and Coach Z was ready for a win, fired up with his loud and commanding voice. I looked over to see where my family was sitting. Will, Nana, and Mom were all the way up, sitting in the top row. Will started blowing his horn at me. I widened my eyes at him to stop. Nana and Mom waved at me and then Mom grabbed the horn out of Will's hands. I quickly waved back and then joined the rest of the team. We huddled together for one last team talk before the clock started and then we began to chant.

"Fight! Fight! Fight! Win! Win! Win!" everyone yelled out together.

Dad came over to me and gave me knuckles. "Let's go! Find it from within. You've got to want it."

I nodded my head at him, so he knew I understood. Jayden was walking out to the field and I ran behind him.

"Hey!" I yelled, trying get his attention.

Jayden turned around and we jumped up and chest bumped each other. It's what we always did, whenever we made a good play or started a game. As the first play began, I was looking all around, taking it all in. I knew it was my time to shine. I watched Jayden and began to run. He threw a perfect pass and I jumped up and caught it. Landing on my feet, I took off and made the touchdown. I had never pumped my arms so fast or weaved in and out of the line with such ease. It felt so good. There was nothing better than that feeling. *Yes! I did it. I got the first touchdown of the season.* The crowd shouted and cheered, I could hear Will blowing his horn, and the announcer yelled out my name.

"Frankie Smith for the touchdown!"

The rest of the team came up and patted me on the back. I high-fived them all.

"Good job blocking," I said.

By the end of the first half, we were up 18-6. Jayden's arm was better than ever. Coach Z called us in to discuss his plan on keeping up the momentum.

"Good job, guys. I want you to try the play that we did yesterday. Sebastian, I want you to take the ball. You ready? Psyche them out."

"Yes, Coach," Sebastian answered back confidently.

"Hu-rah! Hu-rah! Hu-rah!" we yelled.

To admit that I was a little nervous doing the fake out, was an understatement. *What if I mess it up?* Jayden winked at me and before I knew it, everyone was coming my way. I tucked my hand to make it look like I was carrying the ball and got tackled to the ground. They got up and the opposing coach started screaming.

"That way. Get down the field. He's got the ball!"

We pulled it off. Sebastian was in the end zone with a full smile, doing a victory dance, moving his legs side to side.

"*YES!*" I yelled. I got up off the ground and wiped myself off.

Play after play, we kept them on their toes and held the score to our advantage. As the time dwindled down to zero, we knew it was ours to win.

After the game, we celebrated by eating ice cream at the concession stand. Will, Nana, and Mom came over to congratulate me.

"Winner, winner, chicken dinner," Will said jokingly.

He is so embarrassing. I smiled and rolled my eyes, trying to ignore him. Focusing on something else, I got up to greet my grandma.

"Hi, Nana," I said.

"Hi, sweetheart. You played perfectly," she said sweetly. She leaned over and gave me a kiss on my cheek.

"Thank you for coming," I said.

Sebastian butted in. "Thank goodness that play worked out. I thought I was going to throw up, I was so nervous. My cousin Bradley told me I wouldn't be able to pull it off, because I'm too awkward."

Nana put her hand on Sebastian's shoulder. "Your cousin Bradley should believe in you a little bit more. You did wonderful."

"Well, I'm not as good as some of the other kids on the team, and I do get teased sometimes because I'm clumsy and they say I'm heavy-footed. I'm bigger than most of them, so I stand out."

"What's wrong with that? I think that's great. If they want you to be different or they are making fun of you, then they are not your real friends. I see many great traits and I just met you. I like that you are bigger. Just wait until they can't do some of the things that you can. They are going to need your help," Nana said.

"Yeah, remember what Mr. Potter said yesterday? Be your own person. Everyone has their own weirdness about them. It makes you special," I said.

"Who is Mr. Potter?" Mom asked, joining the conversation.

"Yeah, who is Mr. Poooooooter?" Will asked, making fun of me.

I gave him a look of annoyance.

"Will, that's enough. Remember what I told you. If you have nothing nice to say, say nothing at all," Mom said.

Will made a goofy face and walked off to find Dad, who was sitting down with Coach Z, eating BBQ and going over the game.

"Mr. Potter was our substitute yesterday. He had a crazy hat and a bunch of magic tricks and stuff," Sebastian blurted out.

"Yeah, he was pretty cool," I added.

"Magic tricks, huh?" Nana said with curiosity.

"I wish every day was like that," I said.

"Sounds like he made an impression," Mom said.

Jayden and his family came over by us and said hello. Jayden sat down next to me.

"Hey, guys. Hi, Teddy. How are you?" I asked.

"Good. That was a great game. You played awesome," he said.

"Thanks," I said. Smiling, I offered him the seat next to me, so he could sit with us.

Teddy smiled and sat down. Jayden's Mom nodded her head happily that we were including him and went up to get food. Jayden's Dad started talking to my mom about how much time has gone by, and how it was hard to imagine that we were in our last year of youth football.

"Do you remember when they were in flag?" he asked.

"I sure do. They were so cute," my mom answered.

Nana leaned over and whispered in my ear, "Honey, I'm tired. I'm going to go home. I will see you at your next game. Maybe you can come by for dinner one night and spend time with this old lady?"

"Spaghetti and meatballs?" I asked, hoping she would say yes.

"I can whip some up for us," she said, winking at me. "We can watch that game show you like."

"K. Love you," I said.

Nana walked over to Mom and signaled that she was walking to the car. Then, Mom waved at everyone.

"Frankie, I will see you at home. Dad will drive you. I am going to bring Nana home and take Will out to lunch."

"Bye," I said.

We sat there for a while talking and watching the next game. Teddy was getting more comfortable with us and he was beginning to lighten up. He was laughing and telling jokes. Dad walked over to see if I was ready to go home. I picked up my bag and headed toward the truck.

I turned around and yelled. "Bye, guys."

"Bye, Frankie!" Jayden and Teddy yelled back.

Dad put his arm around my shoulder.

"Frankie, I noticed you didn't play with any fear today and it paid off," Dad said.

"I stopped thinking so much," I said.

"Good, keep it up."

As we drove home, I thought about how much time I spent worrying about losing and making mistakes; about what other people would think and disappointing my coach and parents if I wasn't a hundred percent. It was silly, because I know I can't control everything, and worrying won't win games. Comparing myself to others only holds me back. All I can do is try my hardest and be confident, and the rest will fall into place.

CHAPTER 6: BACK TO SCHOOL

"Good morning, class. Sounds like you had a very exciting second day of school. I hope you had a good weekend. It's a beautiful Monday morning. I have heard from many of you about Mr. Potter and how much you enjoyed his teaching. I will have to request him more."

"Yeah. He was awesome. He works at the space museum. We will probably get to see him when we go on the field trip," said Austin.

"That would be fun. Maybe he will be our tour guide. I will put a note in our file to see if he can be with our class," Mrs. Webber said.

"I want to see what kind of hat he wears when he works there. I bet it's really funny," said Amanda.

"He wears fun hats?" Mrs. Webber asked inquisitively.

"Yes. Just like a wizard," Bobby said, laughing. He looked around the room and everyone smiled.

"Sounds interesting. I guess I need to wear more hats if it gets a response like that. I also see that we had some activity over the weekend. We have new frogs. The babies I knew about, but where did this adult frog come from?" she asked.

I clenched my teeth, hoping she would have a good response. Then, I raised my hand.

"I found him in my yard and I wanted to show you, so I brought him to school in a box on Friday. When I saw that we had a substitute, I didn't know what else to do and I didn't want to get in trouble, so I put him in the tank. I'm sorry."

"That's okay, Frankie. Next time, just put him back outside if I am not here. Unfortunately, I have to make sure the other frogs are up for a new one before introducing him. Knowing there are baby frogs, you never know how a new one will act. Sometimes they can eat other frogs. Luckily, this one hasn't."

"Oh. I'm sorry," I said, frowning.

"I like that you brought him in to see me. I love that you are out discovering in nature, finding different creatures. Remember, we can look and release," she reminded.

"Okay," I grumbled, hanging my head low.

"You are not going to give Frankie consequences?" Jenna asked surprised.

Mrs. Webber scrunched her nose and shook her head no. I was happy to hear her reply. I raised my head and smiled at her.

"Mrs. Webber, are you feeling better?" I asked, trying to be nice.

"Frankie, I feel like a brand-new person. Thank you for asking. I had the dreaded stomach flu. There must have been a virus going around. I was here with Mrs. Shubby late a couple nights, setting up the classrooms and getting everything ready for your first day of school. We both must have caught something because we had the same symptoms. So strange."

"Mrs. Shubby had an interesting sub too," Seraphina said, laughing, thinking about his Australian accent.

"I heard he was a little hard to understand," Mrs. Webber implied.

"He was hilarious. We couldn't understand anything he was saying," Bobby exclaimed.

"Next time, just ask him what he is trying to say," she suggested.

"Mr. Potter told us to accept him for who he is and not to make fun of him or say bad things because he is different than us," I said.

"I agree with Mr. Potter. Every teacher has something special to bring to the classroom. I'm sure if you thought back on the last four years of elementary school, you can find differences in all your teachers." Mrs. Webber stated.

"Yes. I loved Ms. Juniper from first grade. She was the nicest teacher I have ever had. I miss her soooo much," Seraphina babbled.

"Mr. Z is the best," Jayden proclaimed.

"That's exactly what I mean. We each have a different way of doing things. It's no different than all of you. Every single student is unique and special. All of you learn at your own pace and it's my job to figure out what works. For instance, some of you are visual learners, you need to see it in front of you. Others learn from listening. Mr. Potter came in and used what he is good at to capture your attention, getting you to learn through demonstration and magic. I have zero knowledge on magic tricks, unless I watch a video and try and teach myself, so I will take a different approach. But I will try to get the same reaction," Mrs. Webber expressed.

"We can teach you a few tricks. He showed us a couple beginner ones, and I bought a magic set over the weekend that I've been practicing on," Landon said.

"I would love that. Maybe we can do that in study hall, or when we have free minutes between subjects. He really inspired you. I'm glad you found a new passion project, Landon."

Mrs. Webber smiled and then turned toward the whiteboard.

"Today, I want to start something with you that we will do every Monday morning. I call it Open Sharing. With all of you going to the middle school next year, it is important to be open and honest and feel safe in here to communicate what you are feeling, what changes you are going through (in here and at home), and any concerns you may have. Anything you want to share that is appropriate can be brought up. Then, when we are done sharing out loud, I want you to take out a piece of paper and write down anything that's on your mind. Put the piece of paper inside the white bucket that I have sitting on the front table. Don't worry, what you write will be anonymous. This will help you clear your mind. You are all getting older. Emotional and social well-being is just as important as your education."

"What if we don't have anything to say?" Mackenna asked.

"I don't have feelings," Bobby declared.

"Sure you do, Bobby. Mackenna, just try it. I won't force any of you. Who would like to start?" Mrs. Webber asked.

Seraphina raised her hand. "My cousin received a scholarship and moved to New York. I miss her."

"That is hard. I have many family members that I don't see as much, the busier we all get. I try and call, email, and text whenever I can to stay in contact. Maybe you can pick a day during her next school break and plan an activity to do with her. Then, you will have something set in stone and you can look forward to it. Also, you can look to your cousin for advice and inspiration as you pass through this year, since you will be moving to another school as well."

Carlos raised his hand. "My parents were gone all weekend. I had a babysitter. It stunk like rotten mushrooms."

"Rotten mushrooms, huh? I guess I know what not to get you for your birthday this year." Mrs. Webber started giggling.

The class burst into laughter.

"Moms and Dads have a lot going on. I am sure they missed you a lot and are happy to be home. Sometimes when our parents are gone, it's a great time to realize all the things they do for us and appreciate them." Mrs. Webber winked at Carlos. "Does anyone else have anything to share?" she asked.

No one raised their hand.

"Okay, take a minute and fill out your piece of paper and put it in the bucket. The first few times we do this, it might feel a little strange, and you may not have much to say, but once you are used to it, many of you will have plenty of things to discuss. However, there is no pressure on what to say. If you want to tell me what you ate this weekend, that's fine. I just want to build our communication."

"Macaroni!" Bobby screamed.

Mrs. Webber squinted her eyes and tilted her head. "Volume control, please. Also, I said to please write it down. Thank you very much."

One by one, we walked up to the bucket and threw our paper pieces into it and then returned to our seats. On the way back to my desk, I stopped Jayden and Teddy.

"Do you guys want to sleepover this weekend?" I asked.

Jayden nodded his head yes. Teddy looked surprised that I included him.

"Sure, yeah…okay. Who else are you inviting?" Teddy asked.

"Maybe Sebastian? Who else do you guys want?" I asked curiously.

"Not Ben," Jayden said, looking at Teddy.

"No. It's okay. Ben can come. We are fine now. He was talking to me this morning. I'm not afraid of him. He won't mess with me. He's actually kind of funny when he's not being mean," Teddy said confidently.

I liked Teddy's new confidence.

"I will ask everyone at lunch. Maybe they can come and hang out for a while but then just you two can spend the night?" I suggested.

"The three amigos," Jayden said.

Teddy smiled. I could tell he liked that. It was no longer just Jayden and I, it was now Jayden, Teddy, and me. It didn't matter that Teddy didn't like sports as much as we did. We did things he liked, and he did things we liked.

"Maybe you can invite Claire and some of her friends," Teddy suggested, teasing me.

I shook my head no and side smiled. "She's got a cheerleading competition."

Mrs. Webber shushed us and told us to go to our seats. She grabbed a workbook and stood in front of us with her teeth clenched.

"It is time for Math. Our first lesson. Who is as excited as I am? We are going to start with decimals and then we will move on to fractions. I want to do a pre-test just to see where we are all at."

Mrs. Webber started to hum a tune and began singing in a high soprano voice.

"Decimals and fractions, multiplication and division, if you follow my lead, you will love math and learn it with precision!" Mrs. Webber started laughing as everyone stared at her with big eyes. "Did you like that little jingle? I just made it up right now."

"Were you in chorus, Mrs. Webber?" Jenna wondered.

"Yes, I was. And I used to do Theatre. Can you believe it? Me…on stage. It seems so long ago," Mrs. Webber said.

"You have a very pretty voice, even if you *were* singing about math facts," Amanda said, while laughing.

Bobby, Carlos, Austin, and Grace put their heads down on their desks, huffing and puffing.

"I know math is not your favorite, but what if I can change that? I have many fun games and activities to get you involved. I even put some of my instructions on video this year, so you have reference materials when you are not with me at school. There are rhymes, riddles, and songs to help you memorize important lessons. Go on our class website and download the video for the week. I go through the lesson and I explain most of the common questions that I usually get. If you still don't understand, you may submit questions to my inbox or leave it on the class message board. I usually get back to you, but if I can't for some reason, I will address it the next day. I just ask that you at least try and figure it out on your own before you come in. Trust me, if you open your mind, you will be amazed at how much you can learn," Mrs. Webber said.

"Math is *soooooo* hard. We don't even use fractions in real life," Bobby complained.

"Sure, we do. Have you ever baked a cake? You need to have specific measurements," Mrs. Webber said.

"Do I look like I bake?" Bobby asked with attitude.

"I don't think bakers have a look. Anyone can do it," Mrs. Webber stated, winking at him.

"To get back on track, math can be difficult, but it is supposed to be. Once it clicks, it's great fun. Let's go back to our previous conversation concerning different teachers and subs for a moment. When Mr. Potter was here, he taught you a few things and you were intrigued by him and his magic tricks, because he made the material relevant and exciting. I won't use magic, but I will make it appealing. If Mr. Potter taught you about chemicals from a textbook, you may not have remembered it at all. Since he made it into a science experiment, creating rainbow colors and fire, you were interested. We need to learn by listening and reading, but we also need to be hands-on. I can do the same thing in math, breaking fractions down, creating groups, and using props to sort things. Okay?"

Mrs. Webber looked at all of us to see our reaction. We shook our heads yes.

"Okay!" we yelled.

Mrs. Webber passed out the pre-test and set the timer.

"You may get started."

Putting my pencil to the paper, I moved quickly through the first page. It was mainly a review from last year. Most of the test was easy, but there were a few things on the last page that I didn't know. I flipped over my paper as I finished the last problem and put my pencil down. Most of the class was still working. Mrs. Webber came over to my desk and picked up my paper.

"Done?" she asked.

I shook my head yes.

"Go ahead and read," Mrs. Webber whispered.

I pulled out a book that I rented from the library about dragons and opened it to the first page. Mrs. Webber backtracked and kneeled next to my desk.

"I forgot to ask you, how was your football game?" she asked quietly.

"Good. We won," I said with a smile, whispering back.

"I wanted to come and watch you guys, but I didn't want to get anyone sick. I will catch one of your next games. Proud of you. Glad you had fun."

As Mrs. Webber walked away, I got a big grin on my face. She was the nicest teacher and I was so happy to have her back. She cared about us, and I knew that I could be myself around her.

Fifteen minutes later, the timer went off. Mrs. Webber walked up and down the aisles.

"Please turn your papers over. Frankie, will you go around and collect them all. You can put them on my desk. We are going to do XtraMath on our computers while I grade them, so I can see what groups to put you in. We will combine with Mrs. Shubby's class, so some of you will be in here and some of you will be in there."

"I want to be in Mrs. Shubby's class. Jeff is in there," Carlos said.

"Sebastian is in there too," Jayden yelled out.

"I know some of your other friends are in there. That's another enticing thing about Math. Also, before we move on, I wanted to tell you quick, before you get started, that I really enjoyed your Genius Hour work that you turned in. There are some very interesting projects going on. Good job on using your imagination and researching topics. I was pleasantly surprised when I saw them."

"Are you going to tell us if our idea was approved or not?" Phil asked.

"Yes. I will pass them out on Friday. I wrote a few comments and I will leave a couple questions for you to think about."

"Mrs. Webber, what subject do we have after Math?" Macayla asked.

"After math, we have specials. Today, you have health and then gym class. You will go straight to recess and lunch and when you come back, we are going to do social studies. Our first lesson is about The Great Pyramids and Egypt. Then, we will watch a video on current news topics. After that, we will move on to writing, where you will write your own family recipe. You are going to research the ingredients and write out the instructions. Lots to do today. Get started on your math, so we can finish up." Mrs. Webber sat down at her desk and let us work on our own.

Everyone pulled out their computers and began to practice level by level. XtraMath gives timed practice tests with three seconds to answer each question. We are supposed to do multiplication and division, to make sure our fluency is good. I whipped through the questions with ease, and was finished again, before most of the class. I didn't ask Mrs. Webber, I just took my book back out. She was checking her calendar and looking something up on her computer.

Ten minutes later, almost everyone had their computers closed and they were waiting for instruction from Mrs. Webber on what to do.

"Mrs. Webber, almost everyone is done. Should we do something?" Kristin asked.

"I think most of you have the right idea. Reading is always a good choice. Now that you are big fifth graders, I think you can make wise choices on your own. You know what I expect."

Kristin pursed her lips and pretended taking selfies.

"I don't think that's what she meant," Amanda said to Kristin.

Kristin started laughing. It was almost time to go to health class. I put my book away and got up to put my water in my lunch bag. Everyone started to line up, following my lead.

Mrs. Webber startled me as she started talking, walking towards the doorway.

"Class, I will definitely reach out to Mr. Potter again. I sent him an email thanking him and letting him know how popular he was. If he can't make it back on my next day off, I have another lady in mind that I think you will love just as much. My niece talks about her all the time. She had her a few times last year and always enjoys her so much," Mrs. Webber said.

"What's her name?" Jayden asked.

"Oh goodness…it was just on the tip of my tongue. I'm trying to remember. It's a peculiar name, that I don't hear often…Mrs. Wa…"

Mrs. Webber put her hand over her eyes and forehead to try and concentrate.

"Ummm…"

"Is it Mrs. Watussi? Mr. Potter told us about her," Amanda said.

"Yes. That's it. Mrs. Watussi. Thanks Amanda," Mrs. Webber said happily.

The class started talking in hush hush comments, discussing what Mr. Potter mentioned about her.

"Can she do tricks and stuff like Mr. Potter?" Mackenna asked.

"I don't know, you will have to wait and see if you get her. It's a surprise when they come in for the day. I've never met her and neither have you. Like we said, every sub has a unique trait. We will just have to anticipate her arrival and see what hers is."

"I don't want you to be gone, Mrs. Webber," Jenna pleaded and whined.

"I know, Jenna. Good thing I don't need anybody for a while. Next month we have a bunch of meetings, so that's when I will need someone to come in. Any who, who wants to learn about bones and the human body?"

Mrs. Webber grabbed the hand of our class skeleton, that was standing by the whiteboard in the front of the classroom and pretended to dance with it.

She was so funny.

"Mrs. Webber, we didn't know you had such good dance moves," Carlos said.

"There's a lot about me you haven't learned yet. Just wait. You have all year to figure it out."

We all started laughing. I went to the back of the line to be by Jayden and rested against the wall, waiting for everyone to move forward. Bobby bumped into me and I tried to grab something to hold onto. As I reached out in front of me, to grab ahold of the wooden bookcase, something fell to the ground. I bent over and picked it up. My eyes grew wide and I gasped. *Is this what I think it is?* It is Mr. Potter's wand. *Did he leave it here? How can he do his magic tricks without it? Should I return it?* Before anyone could see it, I put it in my pocket and covered the top part with my shirt. I walked towards the health room and then stopped. Everyone else went in, but I couldn't move forward. I was feeling guilty. Mrs. Webber came over to me.

"Frankie, are you okay?" she asked.

I pulled the wand out from my pocket.

"No. I found this in the classroom. I want to keep it, but I know I shouldn't. It's Mr. Potter's wand. He showed it to us on Friday. I know I need to turn it in," I said, looking down at the ground."

"Actually, Mr. Potter wrote me a note. He had such a great day with all of you, and our class was so welcoming, that he wanted to donate it to our room. It made him feel so good that his magic made your day, and it's his way to remind all of you to always be yourself, to be unique, to not take things too seriously, to bring fun to your every day by using your imagination, and to accept everyone just the way they are. Maybe you can practice with it? You can hang onto it, Frankie. Just bring it back and let other people see it. Maybe we will have to incorporate the wand into our learning somehow. I am learning that you guys can teach me as much as I'm teaching you." Mrs. Webber patted my back and told me to go to class.

I gave her a side smile and then walked into Health class to see Mr. Z. Even though I knew Mr. Potter's wand didn't have real magical ability, it felt magical as I held it. I put it back in my pocket, covering it with my shirt so I wouldn't disrupt the lesson. As I looked around and thought of each person in the class, I thought about what made each one of them uniquely special and I understood what Mr. Potter taught us that day; no one is better than anyone else. Being our own kind of weird means embracing ourselves, the good, the bad, the silly, and the unordinary. Together, we make up all different kinds of traits. Instead of focusing on other people's differences, we can accept each other and learn from one another. I'm not like anyone else and that's a good thing. I choose to be different. And I choose to standout. I choose to believe in myself and create my own magic.

AND THE TALES CONTINUE......